When To:

WALK

WAIT

& PRAY

AN URBAN CHRISTIAN NOVEL

ANIKA B. ADDERLY

Palmetto Publishing Group
Charleston, SC

When To: Walk, Wait & Pray
Copyright © 2019 by Anika B. Adderly

All rights reserved
No portion of this book may be reproduced, stored in a retrieval system, or transmitted in any form by any means—electronic, mechanical, photocopy, recording, or other—except for brief quotations in printed reviews, without prior permission of the author.

First Edition

Printed in the United States

ISBN-13: 978-1-64111-353-3
ISBN-10: 1-64111-353-7

Book Dedication

This book is dedicated to my past, which has taught me that man does not have the final say, but my future and my destiny lie in the arms of my Heavenly Father who loves me so much that he helped me turn my tears and sorrow into worship and praise!

Special Dedication

For: AJ

To my beautiful baby boy, you have seen your mother scream, cry, struggle, and be broken, but you have also seen how God has restored, rebuilt and revived our lives. I thank God for you, and no matter how hard life gets my son, always remember to keep Jesus Christ first.

Love you always,
Mommy

A good person leaves an inheritance to their children children
(Proverbs 13 :22). New International Version

Train up a child the way they should go; even when he is old
he will not depart from it
(Proverbs 22:6) King James Version.

I can do all things through Christ which strengthens me
(Philippians 4:13) King James Version.

Acknowledgements

To the strong women who have paved the way for me with their prayers, tears and wisdom. To my Grandmother Susie B. Miller who at a very young age introduced me to Jesus Christ. To my mom Betty Roscoe who has loved me from the beginning even when my eyes couldn't see. To my dad Lawrence Adderly, thank you for being there and for the listening ear. To my sisters and a host of loving aunts and uncles who have taught me to believe in myself and to trust God's timing and not my own. A special thanks to Pastors Charles and Yolanda Roberson and the Mighty Prayer Warriors of Kingdom Life Christian Fellowship for loving on me through the darkest times of my life. To all my family and friends who encourage me to keep going when I felt like giving up.

Thank you!

Introduction

Many might question why I chose to write about such personal and traumatic events that occurred in my life but believe me it wasn't my choice or my desire. Years ago, in my adolescent years I dreamed about writing a book, but I never imagined or believe I could do it. I was always one to keep a journal as long as I could remember. It wasn't until 2016 in the year of RESET that I questioned God and what it is he wanted me to do, I mean, why was I born? We are all born with a purpose in this life and a gift. I remember reading and mediating on God's word one night, and God answered, saying "I want you to witness." I started to laugh because I thought I wasn't worthy enough to witness about God. I mean I talked about him, worshipped him and believe in him wholeheartedly, but this was different. This was God's voice, and this was the gift he gave me. I questioned how could I witness to others when I was having difficulty with my own life. Please understand the years 2015 and 2016 were basically the lowest and darkest periods of my life. And then it came to me write about my pain and how God had brought me out. "But God," I asked, "I don't want everyone to know what I've been through. Some things are shameful and I don't want to rehash the pain." Once again, he answered, "Your story is not for you, but for My Glory."

    I contemplated for a long time and talked to some close friends and family members about my fears of writing about my pain and struggles, but I knew I had to obey the Father. The following Sunday my pastor spoke on "Obeying God's Instructions "Do not be afraid or discouraged, for the Lord will personally go ahead of you. He will be with you; He will neither fail you nor abandoned you" (Deuteronomy 31:8). I couldn't do anything but smile because that sermon was for me and I know for a fact" that God will get our attention whether we want it or not. "Okay, God I hear you," I said. Then I thought about leaving certain things out, and then once again a faint voice whispered, "If you do, I won't bless it." Right then I knew that this was bigger than me.

So, I picked up my many journals and started organizing my words and thoughts. Night after night I prayed, cried and then cried some more, but I kept going, and now it's complete. My focus shifted from trying to please my then-husband, family and friends, to pleasing God. I had to change my circle and my way of thinking. A lot of friends became fewer friends and guess what, I am fine with that. Believe me, not everyone will get you or understand you, but it's okay. Stay the course, stay focused and finish the race. "The race is not given to the swift nor to the strong, but he who endures until the end." (Ecclesiastes 9:11) It took me a long time to understand that verse completely and now it's one of my favorite scriptures.

So, this is my story, my blood, sweat, tears, and adversities. My personal testimony of how magnificent our God can be if we allow him to lead the way. This book is written to inspire you, challenge you and to encourage you. It might bring some tears and laughter too, but believe me we all have a story. Yours might be different from mine or it may be similar, but I'm here to remind you that you, my friend, are strong, beautiful and special.

While writing this book I asked God to send strong powerful people into my life that would help elevate me, push me, and open doors for me, but more important pray for me and with me. And guess what ya'll, he did! And then I asked him to reveal and remove anyone that would hinder me or my walk, and guess what ya'll? He did that too! In this walk I've realized that everyone cannot go with you. If you want your destiny and the promises of God to prevail in your life, please know you will be tested and tried beyond what you can imagine, but it's how you overcome these obstacles and tests that determines your purpose. So, my dear loved one, if I can overcome these burdens, humiliations, trials and hurdles life has thrown my way, then so can you!

Blessings to you all,
Anika

CHAPTER 1
Quiet Moments

Symone sat there feeling jubilant and blessed as she watched her ten-year-old son Jordan cross the stage graduating from fifth grade. The joy that he brought to her life could not be explained. When Symone was seventeen years old the doctor informed her that she would never be able to have children, but due to God's grace and mercy, He had other plans for her life. Jordan was the apple of his mother's eye, a high-spirited, energetic, loving God-fearing young man. Tears of joy rolled down Symone cheeks as she watched her baby boy begin a new chapter in his life.

Jordan and Symone had been through a lot together, more than any mother would want her child to endure. She prayed daily that the foolishness and violence that her son had witnessed between his parents over the years would somehow dissipate from his life. Symone would pray daily that her husband's insecurities, infidelity and temper tantrums would not take root in their son. She had witnessed the hurt and betrayal in her husband's eyes for years, his pain of being neglected by his parents at such a young age, and that same anger and fear still lived in him as an adult to this day.

Symone had done all she could for her marriage, and now she was finally at peace...a certain kind of peace that surpassed all understanding. She continued to pray for her husband's salvation daily, and fasted, as well, but enough was enough. She couldn't understand why God would allow so much turmoil to enter her marriage. The lies, deceit and betrayal was not what she envisioned as a wife and not what she prayed for as a child. She started to feel that God had turned His back on her.

Symone and Darius's love affair was far from a fairy tale. See, it all began in a combat zone while both of them were deployed. A relationship was the last thing Symone was looking for. Previously she was involved in a heavy relationship with Talik before things went left.

Talik Johnson stood at least six feet three inches with skin as dark, as deep mocha, voluptuous full lips, and the body frame as one of those thick running backs who played professional football. But that beautiful grin could light up any room he entered, and that was one of the things that attracted Symone to him. As a matter of fact, Talik could have been a twin for Idris Elba. Symone and Talik's romance was cut short due to his National Guard Unit being called to active duty, but Symone had decided that there was something there worth waiting for, so she decided to wait. The first couple of months were hard and the communication quite difficult. Sgt. Talik Johnson and his unit had been deployed to a red zone and he couldn't communicate as much as he wanted, so they wrote letters frequently to one another. Symone prayed daily that the good Lord above would protect him and this unit, and that they would not fall into enemy hands. The time had finally come for Symone to deploy, as well. This was her third deployment to Iraq, but she knew that it could always be her last. Symone was a woman of faith and she believed God promises for her life. So therefore, when her country called for her to defend it, she rested assured in the Savior's arms that she would be okay.

Months had passed before she heard from Talik. She was informed from her Chain of Command that Mosul, a nearby camp, had been attacked. Her heart quelled with fear, it was as if her heart had just stopped. No! Talik was stationed in Mosul. She began to weep, for she did not know what had become of him. The only thing she knew to do was pray, pray for his safety and his fellow soldiers. Two weeks later, Symone's commander summoned her to his office. As she entered the room she observed a distraught and sorrowful look on her captain's face.

Sergeant Lockett "Please sit down. I have just received some disheartening information regarding the attack in Mosul."

"Mommy! Mommy!! It's time to take graduation pictures. Do you hear me?"

Jordan's voice brought Symone back to reality instantly. "Yes, baby boy. Mommy hears you. Let's go."

Symone began to get choked up all over again as she watched her son beam with happiness as he stood there in his graduation cap and gown. *Wow! My baby boy is growing up into a fine young man.* Symone closed her eyes and softly whispered a prayer to the Heavenly Father Above.

"Dear Precious Father, thank you for bringing Jordan into my life, I know I have made mistakes in my life, but I pray that you never remove your hand from his life, and please guide him in all his ways. Amen."

After pictures were taken, Jordan couldn't remain still. Not only did he graduate from fifth grade, but he left his elementary school achieving the high honor roll. In a subdued tone Jordan asked his mother, "Why didn't Daddy come to my graduation? Did he forget?"

Symone could hear the heart and trembling of his words, and knew her son was trying to fight back his tears as hard as he could, but eventually the tears started to flow down his caramel chubby cheeks. "Honey, I don't know, but best believe I will find out."

Symone could not believe the audacity of her soon-to-be ex-husband not showing up to his baby boy's graduation. She couldn't wait until their final divorce date. She could not believe the man Darius had become. After so many prayers and asking God for guidance pertaining to this marriage, she had eventually learned to rest and not worry, and let God take control, as she had so many times before.

CHAPTE 2
The Girl Loves Diamonds

Alani tossed and turned all night long. Tears soaked her satin pillow case and sheets. She could not believe what had just transpired. Nearly fourteen hours prior, Mykal had escorted Alani to one of South Beach's finest restaurants, The Forge. The entire day had been mesmerizing. Mykal called Alani at work and told her he would be waiting for her downstairs when she got off. Alani didn't know what was going on, but she knew she liked the sound of an exciting evening. At six o'clock precisely, she rushed down the corridor to the bottom floor, and there stood Mykal dressed in a cream light-weight button-down double-breasted Armani suit. Her heart started to tingle at the very sight of this amazing, gorgeous man.

There Mykal stood, six feet one, dark as a pot of freshly brewed coffee, and skin as smooth as a baby's bottom. "Hello, my beautiful Nubian Queen. We have exactly three hours before our reservation, and please do not ask any questions. Just let me be your King of the night for this evening." He continued to stand before her, gleaming with those beautiful white teeth and curvaceous delicious lips smiling. "But Mykal I have to go home and shower."

"Oh no, baby girl, I got everything lined up for you, so let's go. Time wasted is time lost remember?" Alani was puzzled but she went with the flow. Approximately fifteen minutes later they pulled into Mykal's sister Tori's beauty salon. "Okay, baby girl, I will be back in two hours. Follow Tori's instructions without asking any questions."

As Alani entered the salon, there stood Tori, who greeted her with a kiss on the cheek. "Hey girl we have two hours to get you ready, and a team of hair and make-up artists waiting on you, so let's get started."

Alani rushed upstairs to Tori's apartment for a quick shower and back downstairs for hair and make-up. Alani got caught up in the excitement until she remembered she didn't have anything to wear for the evening.

Tori must have sensed Alani's worries. "Oh girl, don't worry I got that covered too."

Two hours later, Mykal arrived as he had promised. After entering his sister's salon, there he stood speechless as Alani came before him in a one-shoulder champagne silk chiffon double split thigh-high goddess design. He couldn't believe how beautiful Alani was, but not only was she a beautiful woman on the outside she was even more beautiful on the inside. Mykal knew that he wanted the best for her and perhaps he was falling in love with her...but he could never have her because of his lifestyle. He cared for her more than any other woman he had ever been with, and he had been with quite a few in his line of work. But tonight was all about Alani, for tomorrow had enough trouble of its own. Exactly forty-five minutes later, Mykal and his beautiful date pulled into The Forge. Mykal and Alani dinned by candlelight. The restaurant was most exquisite. The large crystal chandelier was the center attraction of the entire room. Mykal kept the Dom Perignon flowing throughout the night, for he knew that was Alani's favorite. Mykal knew he had to make up for that scene he'd caused outside her friend's home two weeks ago. He felt terrible for what he did to her, and in front of her best friend, for he knew she was totally humiliated and ashamed by his actions.

You see, early that Tuesday morning Mykal had received a phone call that he had been waiting on for at least six months. This new client would open many doors for Mykal that he never would have dreamed of—a door to unlimited possibilities. After agreeing to his new client's terms. Mykal felt that he was untouchable. Money meant power to Mykal, and the more money the more powerful you would become. And that's exactly what he yearned to have—power in the streets of Miami.

While riding down the South Florida coast he decided to treat himself to something new, and what better way to celebrate than bling? With his new contacts he knew he could afford it, and whatever else his heart desired.

Mykal love to listen to hardcore gangster rap, but today he felt like listening to something different. As he was flipping through the radio stations with his new auto remote, he stumbled upon a familiar voice. It was Dr. Tony Evans. Tony Evans was one of Alani's favorite pastors, and being with Alani was how he was introduced to Pastor Evans. Mykal was intrigued about the topic that was currently being discussed, which was "The Battle of the Mind." Mykal listened intensively, for he was caught up in a battle, a battle for the streets and power. He knew what he was doing was wrong and immoral, but he couldn't help it, for he loved to make money. He knew that judgment day would come, but hopefully it wouldn't be today.

Mykal pulled into one of Miami's most distinguished jewelers. This was not your everyday jewelry store. This place was over the top and highly protected. Once you entered the building you had to be buzzed in, and there was a security scan for all customers. Only the wealthiest could afford to shop here. Once entering the facility, one had to show their I.D. and access was granted to enter the second door, which lead to the jewelry floor. Mykal's face lit up once he saw all those colored jewels. Twenty-karat and eighteen-karat gold, rubies, pink and black diamonds, and jewels in almost every color that one could ever imagine. As Mykal looked around for something that caught his eye, he stumbled across a stunning Cartier necklace. This necklace was like no other. It was adorned with emeralds and diamonds—such beauty and style. Only one name came to mind who could wear such a precious piece.

Later that night he presented the gift to Alani. She cried, for she had never seen anything so beautiful as this necklace. She knew that inside the hard, stern man who many feared was a loving, adoring gentle giant who was eagerly waiting to get out, and one way or the other she was going to bring him to the surface for all to see. Alani knew that one way or the other, she was going to change him for the better. After Mykal placed the necklace on Alani's long, slim neck, he warned her that it was not an everyday piece, but priceless. Therefore he only wanted her to wear it when they were together. Alani was still mesmerized by the exquisite piece, so at this point she agreed to Mykal's request, but in the back of her mind she knew that she had to show it off at least once to one of her friends.

It had been over two weeks since Mykal had given Alani her gift, and yet she still was gleaming from the inside out. She thought to herself how much he must care for her, for only wives would get something as remarkable or expensive as that. Oh! Maybe that was it! *Mykal has fallen in love with me. Wow!* The thought of that idea made her even more excited about the possibility of marrying such a man. Alani had just bought a new outfit and she knew that her necklace would be the perfect finishing touch. With that, Alani decided to wear her gift to work that morning. As she walked into her office, she couldn't but notice the stares coming from her co-workers. See, Alani knew that the gossip would soon start through the work environment that the guy she was dating was a drug dealer, but at this point she didn't care. Not only was she wearing a diamond and emerald-studded Cartier necklace that she later got appraised at six thousand dollars, but today she wore a V neck low-cut hunter-green silk wrap blouse with a black pencil fitted ankle-length skirt accessorized with her emerald-green open-toed Blanco shoes. Alani felt good and smelled like new money...if this what new money felt like. And being married to Mykal, she couldn't wait.

Once she got situated at her desk, she began to file the reports that were due to her boss tomorrow. Alani worked as a secretary for a large department store in South Florida. Even though it was a decent job to have at the age of twenty-three, she knew that there was more to her life. After reviewing her notes before she submitted the file to her boss, she received an urgent call from her friend Tyree on her cell. Tyree was crying so hysterically that Alani couldn't understand a word she was saying. The only thing that she could piece together was, "He is Out!"

Alani informed her boss that she will be taking an early break and that her report would be completed by the end of the day. Thirty minutes later, Alani pulled into her friend's apartment complex. As she came closer, she saw Tyree sitting on the stoop in front of her complex building. Mens clothing was thrown all over the lawn, and only one guess who they belonged to. Tyree's no-good trifling baby-momma-drama live-in boyfriend Tony. Only if Tyree could find someone else better than Tony, her life would be so much better. Tyree was a beautiful woman and many men were drawn to her beauty, for she stood at five foot seven and one hundred seventy pounds with a thick banging body and beautiful hazel eyes. But she only had eyes for Tony. Tony wasn't a bad looking guy by any means. A little on the slim side for Alani. He wore his hair short and taped with deep waves that made you seasick just looking at him.

As Alani cut the engine off and got out the vehicle, her friend rushed into her arms crying her heart out. Once again she mumbled that Tony was still cheating and lying, but the hardest part was that a child had been conceived this time. After living together for three years she'd found out about the baby, and the child had just turned two. Tyree revealed to Alani that earlier that morning a girl named Dory had stopped by their apartment with her son TJ. Dory admitted that she and Tony had been off and on for seven years, and the reason for their breakup was that she had refused to have another abortion. She had already had two, and she promised herself and God that she would never kill another child. Tony and Dory had crossed paths four years ago, and once again a child was conceived. After she refused to have an abortion he walked out. Dory admitted that she loved Tony and wanted him in TJ's life, but all he wanted was sex, and she had enough of his lies.

As Alani became to comfort her friend, her phone began to ring. Oh no, she forgot about her lunch date with Mykal.

"Hey beautiful. Where are you?"

"Hey handsome. I'm sorry sweetie, I took an early lunch break to come see about my friend Tyree. She and Tony had another fight."

"All right," Mykal replied, "but remember their business is theirs and not ours, understand?"

"Yes, I know, but that's my friend and she needed me."

"Hey, isn't that your friend that stays off 64st in the Gables?"

"Yes, that's her."

"Okay, well I'm just finishing up some business not too far from there. I would love to put my eyes on you before you go back to work and maybe I can sneak in a kiss? You know how I feel about you Alani. Believe me this is straight talk and not a game."

Alani began to blush like a little school girl with her first crush. "All right then baby, I'll see you in a few and be careful."

"I will," Mykal responded.

Once Alani hung up with Mykal, she turned her attention back to her friend Tyree who was soaked in her tears and in pain once again from the acts of betrayal. "Girl, I'm sorry I forgot Mykal and I had plans for lunch."

"It's okay Alani. I appreciate you coming by and I'm happy you and Mykal are doing well. I take it you're starting to develop serious feelings for him."

"Yeah girl, I can't believe how well he treats me."

"That's all good Alani, but let's not forget what he does for a living."

"Please! Let's not go there Tyree," Alani responded, quite irritated from the comment.

"I'm sorry girl. If he makes you happy then I'm all in, and from what I see around your neck he's all into you, as well."

Oh no! Alani forgot she was wearing her new Cartier diamond necklace. She could only hope that Mykal wouldn't be too upset with her because she broke that promise.

Just then, Mykal pulled up in his new diamond-white Jaguar x30 convertible. As Mykal pulled up into the complex, she decided to go meet him. She was so happy and couldn't wait to embrace him, but as she approached closer she saw the look of confusion written all over his face. Better yet, it seemed to be more anger than anything. Mykal's eyes weren't on Alani, but on what was around her neck.

"Alani didn't I tell you that this was not to be worn as an everyday piece? This set me back quite a few stacks, and all I asked was for you to respect my feelings and to keep your promise. And damn, from the looks of it you can't even do that."

Alani had never heard this tone from Mykal before. It was quite frightening and very stern, and she did not appreciate it at all. Before she could try to explain herself, Mykal immediately snatched the necklace off her neck, turned his back, and left as quickly as he'd come. Alani stood there looking dumfounded. She couldn't believe what just had taken place before her very own eyes. She had never seen this side of Mykal. For this was the side of Mykal that many men feared, but also the man that she had grown so fond of and started to love.

Tyree then rushed to her friend's side to comfort her. "I'm so sorry Alani. I can't believe he did that to you."

Alani stood there frozen as if she had just seen a ghost. Perhaps it was a ghost she never wanted to cross.

CHAPTER 3

See the Vision

After an exciting day of celebration, shopping, shedding tears and eating pizza, Symone was exhausted. As soon as she and Jordan pulled into their new two-story brick home Jordan asked if he could go to his friend Shaun's house and show him his new awards.

"Sure, thing honey, not a problem, but I want you home within an hour okay?"

"Thanks Mom," and he was off running across the beautiful manicured lawn.

Symone couldn't wait to take a refreshing bubble bath in her new jacuzzi tub. At this point the only things she needed to make this bath perfect was to light some candles, a glass of chardonnay, and the soothing sounds of Alonzo Blackwell playing in the background. As soon as Symone stepped onto her wooden mahogany floors her phone began to ring. After seeing Darius's number, she sent it automatically to voicemail. She was not in the mood to deal with another blatant lie or a lame excuse from Jordan's dad. Symone was still overjoyed about her new home and how God had opened another window for her and her son.

Soon after Symone and Darius separated she moved back into her home, but she knew that there was more for her, and although she loved her home it reminded her too much of Darius. Every room held a memory from her past, whether it was good or bad, and she knew that she had to start over fresh. Symone always dreamed of having a larger home, perhaps a two-story brick house, four bedrooms and three and a half bathrooms, and of course a gourmet kitchen, as well, for Symone knew how to cook. Owning a larger home was never important to Darius. He was settled living in his house. But Symone wanted more for her life and her son. This is just one of the topics that they could never agree upon. So after the divorce, Symone decided she was going to accomplish her goals that she set for herself, and this time no one would be able to stop her. It was hard working two jobs, going to school and taking business courses, but she knew that greatness was within her, and if it took leaving her husband to discover her destiny, then so be it.

It took some hard work and a lot of dedication on Symone's part, but the time had come for her and Jordan to go house hunting. It was a beautiful summer morning in August when Symone and Jordan went house hunting. They looked all throughout the city of Savannah. Although the homes were lovely they weren't what she had pictured, so then she decided to look on the outskirts of the city. As they were driving through one of the suburbs, Symone came upon a house that resemble a home they had added to their vision board almost two years prior.

"Mommy look, that's the house I saw in my dream!"

Symone looked pretty confused at her son, but she couldn't help to smile at his enthusiasm. "I hear you son, but we must call the Realtor to see when we can look at the house."

"Okay Mom, but I'm telling you, that's our new house!"

Symone giggled under her breath but went ahead to call the Realtor whose information was on the sign and, just her luck, the office was right around the corner, Sharon the Realtor agreed to meet Symone there within the next ten minutes. Honestly, Symone was thrilled that she would be able to view the house. She and Jordan looked at one another and bust out into laughter.

Exactly ten minutes later the Realtor pulled into the driveway of the home. After introducing themselves, Symone and her son were led up the beautiful brick home driveway. Sharon informed Symone that the house had been on the market for some time now and the price was recently lowered by fifteen thousand dollars. That made her even more impressed.

As they entered the foyer they could see the sunlight coming in from all directions of the house, and the crown molding was stunning. The house had four bedrooms, three and a half bathrooms, and two bonus rooms with a three-car garage. The first level was all hardwood floors except for the kitchen. The gourmet kitchen was absolutely stunning. It had vanilla glazed cabinetry, a huge granite center island, a five-burner stove and a wine fridge. This indeed was a dream kitchen.

Next, they made their way up the beautiful wooden staircase. Jordan was so excited about the large house that he went to find his room. Symone and Sharon continued to the master suite, which had a huge walk-in closet and a huge his and hers granite shower. Symone couldn't believe that Jordan was right. This appeared to be the house they added to their vision board and asked God for.

"Momma!" Jordan called, sounding out of breath, "you have got to come see this."

"What is it honey?"

"My room!" he exclaimed. "It's my room!" Jordan grabbed his mom by the hand to lead her to his room. "Look Mom, it has a built-in bookcase and my very own desk. I could do all my homework right here, and in the next room could be my boy cave where me and my friends could hang out."

"Jordan, if you love it so far, wait until you see the backyard," Sharon replied jokingly.

"Okay, I'm ready to go!"

The backyard included a wraparound patio with a custom fire pit, fenced-in yard, and a built-in gas grill, and there was still room for Symone to add a pool if she desired. She knew she wanted this house, but long ago Symone had learned to pray and wait for God to answer.

After thanking Sharon for her hospitality, Symone began to wonder if the price was too much. She had set a price aside, but the asking price was ten thousand more. Symone whispered to herself in a faint tone, "Heavenly Father, this appears to be the home that we've prayed for and the asking price is more than I have. I trust you. I believe in you, and I know you answer prayers. I pray that this home is indeed for me and my son, and that you hear our prayers. Amen."

Four months later, Symone received the call she had been waiting for, her offer for the house was accepted.

After her relaxing bath, Symone decided to watch one of her all-time favorite movies, *One Night with The King*, the story of Queen Esther. Just as she climbed into bed she heard Jordan downstairs in the kitchen.

"Mom, I'm back," she heard her son's voice through the house intercom. "And I brought Chase and Isaiah with me. We will be outside on the patio if you need me."

"Okay, just keep the noise down."

Moments later her cell phone rang again. It was Darius. Symone learned a while ago to pray and ask God to guide her mind, tongue, and spirit when talking to Darius because if He didn't, some harsh words would be spoken.

"Hello Darius. Jordan is downstairs with his friends. I will have him call you back." She felt like going off, but she kept her tone short and firm.

"Symone, I'm sorry I got caught up at work, really," he replied.

"Today was our son's graduation and that's the best you could come up with? Look! I don't care what you were doing or who you were with, but when it comes to our son I would appreciate if you try to put him first."

"Symone! I wasn't with anyone, I set my alarm an hour earlier, but I didn't hear it go off."

"Once again, Darius," Symone replied bitterly, "you failed your son, and of course he was devastated again. But hey, that's just you. The more you disappoint him, the more you continue to push him away. Keep it up and you're going to lose him altogether. I've got to go. I will pass the message along, Darius. Bye." She hung the phone up before he could reply. "He makes me so mad, but never again will I allow anyone to take my peace," she uttered.

Once again, her phone started to ring, but this time it was Darius's mom, Gertrude.

"Oh! Hell, no!" Symone thought to herself. "Not today. Not today…"

CHAPTER 4

I don't Care!

Gertrude was a meddling, vindictive and nosy woman. As a matter of fact, she was the one Symone blamed for a lot of her and Darius's marital problems. Whenever Symone and Darius had an argument he would call his mom, and she in turn would call Symone. It was simply crazy. Symone couldn't tell if Darius was married to her or his mom.

Each conversation with Gertrude started with, "What did you do to my son?" It got so bad Symone told Gertrude to never call her again if it wasn't to speak to Jordan. Symone couldn't believe what a momma's boy Darius had become. She didn't know how she missed it, because he wasn't always like that. Symone believed that whatever happened between a married couple was between them and God, and not the entire darn family. But somewhere in their vows, Darius didn't understand that concept. Symone remember Pastor Reid on their wedding day stating in front of the congregation, "Keep family out of the marriage," and for the family to allow them to be married. As a matter of fact, he declared it and prayed that all would listen. Symone felt that when she said, "I Do" to Darius, but his mother said, "I Don't" and their marriage had been hell ever since. But she couldn't blame Gertrude for everything, because Darius was the one who'd brought her into their marriage.

Symone remembered the first time she met Gertrude, it was right after her sonogram and she and Darius had just found out that they were having a son. Gertrude and his dad, Fred, were visiting from Louisiana.

Darius was so happy that he ran into the house. "Momma! Good news! Symone and the baby are doing just fine and it's a boy."

Fred congratulated his son and both men went outside to have a drink. Symone, Gertrude, and Darius's grandmother, Mabel, were left inside the family room. Coldheartedly, Gertrude whispered, "I already have three grandchildren I don't need another!"

Ms. Mabel shook her head and replied, "Children are a blessing."

Symone couldn't believe what she had just heard. "Well," Symone replied angrily. "Lady, with that attitude, I don't care if you ever see my child!" Then she called for Darius with tears in her eyes. "Please get me out of here!"

Darius drove Symone home, but for the life of him he did not know what had transpired between the two women in his life. Symone was so hurt from hearing such harsh words from this woman. How could anyone utter harsh words to an unborn child, she asked herself? The more she thought about it, the angrier she got. She tried to hold the tears back, but they came, and they did not stop. Darius tried to console her, but at that point she wanted to get far away from him and his mom. As soon as Darius pulled into her driveway, Symone anxiously jumped out the car.

He immediately ran behind her yelling for her to stop. "Symone baby, please tell me what's wrong," Darius pleaded, concerned and worried.

"Ask your mom!" Symone yelled, and shut the door in his face, leaving him to wonder what his mom had said.

CHAPTER 5
Life Lessons

Darius knew Symone would be upset, but he didn't expect her to hang the phone up on him. He hated disappointing his son. He hated what had become of him and Symone. So much negativity, turmoil and a lot of tears. Darius couldn't believe that he was going through the same exact thing as his previous marriages. He seldom wondered how this could be happening again, for he knew that he loved his wife very much, but at times it felt as though the world was against them. Darius knew the biggest mistake he had made was involving his mother in his martial affairs. He knew that upset Symone, and yet he continued to do it out of selfish reasons. However, not only was that an obstacle in their marriage, but the biggest regret was him cheating on his wife.

Darius was known for letting the opinions of others cloud his judgment regarding his marriage and his family, and now his marriage along with his life was in turmoil. He knew that Symone could bring out the best in him, but also the worst. When they were good, they were very good, but when they were bad, all hell broke out. Symone and Darius knew how to bring the best and worst out in each other. Darius always like to plan things ahead, according to his life. If things didn't go as he had hoped, he would become very disgruntled. That is what had happened before, in his last marriage, but he and Symone were different. He knew things would be different this time around.

He often questioned himself. Was he the cause of his failed marriages? or did the fault lie with the women he married? Darius knew he had his issues, but he couldn't believe that he was at this place again in life, and more importantly, at this age. Symone had started to change right before his eyes. Instead of that ride-or-die woman he'd met years ago who wasn't afraid of anyone, including him, she was now becoming a lot more mellow and focusing more on her walk with God and her destiny than the constant arguing and cursing as before. Darius knew God and believed in Christ, but he still wondered about certain things, like why it was so important to give tithes to the church or attend bible study? He couldn't understand why it was so important to Symone that they went to church together or get in the daily habit of praying as a family. He had church in his heart, why did he have to go inside a building and listen to other people's problems? Shoot, he had enough problems of his own. One thing he always remembered Symone saying once they got married, was that it was important for them to pray together and read the bible together, because if they didn't the enemy would come in and destroy their foundation. Now he saw exactly what she'd meant by it. He was the head of the house who had let the enemy destroy his family, and now he didn't know if he would ever get them back.

CHAPTER 6

A Night to Remember

After a memorable night and a romantic moonlight walk on South Beach, Mykal and Alani checked into the luxurious Fontainebleau Hotel. As soon as they entered the room, the soft flickering tea light candles lit the entire room with rose petals spread out on the floor and across the king size bed.

"Mykal my dear, you thought of everything," she said with a grin.

"This is only the beginning, Alani. There is so much more I want to show you."

Alani then melted into his arms, followed by kissing him softly along his neck, for that drove Mykal crazy! Slowly, they eased their way to the king-sized bed where they engaged in intense, passionate lovemaking. Their legs intertwined as one as the beats of their hearts moved together in one rhythm. After an intense night and a long, hot, steamy shower, both decided to stay inside and order room service. Not only did they enjoy teasing and kissing one another, but also the genuine friendship and laughter they shared. After apologizing during dinner for his behavior, Mykal returned the beautiful necklace to Alani, and promised he would never treat her that way again. Once they checked out of the hotel, Mykal decided to end their weekend with a shopping spree. He took Alani to the jeweler where he'd purchased the necklace, and added to her collection a pair of emerald diamond earrings, and for himself a platinum and black diamond Movado watch. He then informed Alani he had a meeting later that afternoon, so once they finished he would take her home and be back at five that evening to continuing celebrating their festivities.

After pulling out of the garage and heading south on I-95, Mykal noticed in the rearview mirror that the same black suburban was following them as he'd noticed earlier that day. He wasn't sure if it was the feds, or one of his new enemies. His new contacts were very dangerous people, and several others were upset that Mykal had join forces elsewhere and not with them. Mykal knew he had enemies, but none of them would dare to threaten him or his new position.

Alani immediately sensed that something was wrong because he started to sweat profusely. "What's wrong, baby?" Alani asked, worried.

He didn't want to alarm her of the danger that they were in, but he knew he had to get her out of there, and quickly. The more Mykal accelerated, the faster the suburban followed. Luckily for Mykal, there weren't a lot of cars that morning on the highway. The suburban was not giving up or slowing down. Then suddenly, there was shooting coming from the suburban.

Alani started screaming to the top of her lungs as Mykal pressed his foot to the floor, going as fast as he could in his convertible to get them to safety.

Alani screamed, crying hysterically, calling on Jesus to save them from this deadly attack.

CHAPTER 7

Reflections

Symone woke up early Saturday morning. Today was the first day of her three day fast.

She remembered as a child her grandmother Bee use to fast all the time, but she never understood the reasoning behind it. But now as an adult, she understood the spiritual meaning of fasting all too well. Symone had been fasting for over three years now. She really didn't start until Pastor Reid asked his congregation to seek God more and deny themselves of the worldly goods, whether it was sex, alcohol, TV, social media, or food. He advised the members that it was time to hear from our Father God, to deny themselves and glorify him.

During that time, Symone and Darius's marriage was at its lowest point, and that was the time she needed to seek God's guidance on her life and their marriage. Some members had decided to do a one week fast from social media, and others chose the Daniel's fast. But Symone was new to it and she wanted to start off slow.

The first day was torture for Symone. Her stomach growled constantly, so she continued to drink her water and chicken broth. During this fast, Symone learned how to feast on the bread of life which was the holy bible, and not the bread her body was accustomed to. The more she focused on reading and mediating on the bible, the better she felt. The second day, she started all over again by giving thanks in prayer, then back to reading the scriptures, followed by meditation. During the quiet times with God, she learned how to let the scriptures penetrate into her spirit and listened for the Holy Spirit to answer. Later that night, Symone began to get discouraged because she had not heard from God. She began to wonder if she was doing something wrong, or if God was truly hearing her prayers, or if he even cared.

The next morning while in prayer, Symone went into her secret place and lay before the Lord weeping. During her fast she began to post scriptures all around her pertaining to her situation. "Father please tell me what to do in this marriage, for I am so tired of the crying and my soul is tired." Symone must have drifted off to sleep in prayer, because when she awoke she remembered a small, faint voice whisper, "You cannot have the marriage you want, until I finish working in Darius."

"But Lord, what about me?" she responded.

"Stay in me, as I will in you." And just like that the voice was gone.

Symone got up from her closet feeling jubilant. "My God has indeed answered my prayers, and he told me what I must do, but how long must I wait God?" she wondered. Symone was so excited that she had heard from God that she called her best friend and sister in Christ, June.

June picked up on the second ring. "Hey girl, I was just thinking about you."

"June! June!" Symone yelled through the phone excitingly. "He spoke to me! God answered my prayer, he told me what I must do."

"I'm so happy for you, Symone," June replied. "It's such a wonderful feeling, isn't it? Didn't I tell you to cast all your cares on the Lord? Symone my dear, 'if you remain faithful God will answer you, but in his timing not yours'" (Psalms 55:22).

"June, it feels as if the weight of the world has been lifted off me."

"Symone, you've contacted the Heavenly Father. Now you must learn how to maintain that communication. For this battle is not yours, but the Lord's. Sweetie, let God handle Darius. You must stand back and let him do it. Symone, now you know well as I do, we cannot fix a man or change him. He's not ours to fix, but the Lord's. That's how so many women get themselves into trouble, thinking they can fix their man. We all are God's children, and he loves us all. Even though we disappoint him daily, he still loves us. One thing I have learned in this walk is that it takes a strong woman and a prayer warrior to continue in the fight. The enemy has been knocking at your door for some time now, and he thinks he's in control. But God is the one who sits on the throne along with Jesus Christ our Lord, and there is where he intercedes for us when we can't. We don't know how the end is going to turn out regarding your marriage, but it will work out for your good in the end, I promise you."

"I know, June, I know, but it's hard."

"Yes, my friend, life doesn't come easy, and if it did would it be a life? I love you, and will continue to pray for you. Also make sure you read (Romans 8:28). Okay, bye, girl."

Symone was so happy June was in her life. Years ago, June and her husband went through a battle of their own, and it was Symone who was there for her. Symone recalled how her friend would come to work, her hair a mess and clothing just thrown together. This was not the vibrant, beautiful, and cheerful woman whom Symone had grown accustomed to. After confiding in Symone about her marital problems and her husband's infidelity, a spiritual sisterhood was formed. That was eight years ago, and when Symone received her divorce papers at work, June was right there to console her and pray with her, as Symone did years prior.

After watching Jordan gobble down his morning breakfast of sausage, cheese grits and waffles, Symone and Jordan prayed before he went off to school. Once he left and kissed his mom on the cheek, Symone went into the study and began to recite and meditate on one of her favorite bible verses.

"He that dwelleth in the secret place of the most High shall abide under the shadow of the Almighty" (Psalms 91 KJV). This verse reminded Symone of God's covering over her life if she dwelt with him, then no evil will overcome her or her household. After retreating into her secret place, she once again lay before the Lord and made her requests known, but not before giving thanks for all He has done in her life and would continue to do.

CHAPTER 8
Farewell

Alani's world with Mykal would never be the same. After God answered her prayer about keeping them safe, Mykal and Alani drove to her condo in complete silence.

Upon entering her place, Mykal sat Alani down with tears in his eyes. "Baby, I could have lost you tonight. I endangered you with my lifestyle, I don't want to think of what could have happened. Please Alani find it in your heart to forgive me. I never wanted this to happen, but I can promise you that it will never happen again. Sweetie, I realize that I am in love with you, and the thought of me not protecting you tonight scares me. But now I know I must put you first because I love you. Being with me is no good for you. I want better for you, and you should, as well. You are indeed a beautiful, intelligent, kind woman and I can't hold you back. I would lose my mind if something were to happen to you because of me. Alani, you have always talked about traveling and seeing the world. I think it would be a great idea if you considered joining the military. That way you could finish your degree, travel the world, and get out of Miami. Not only would you have a great life, but just maybe you will meet a fantastic guy who will love you the way you deserve."

Alani sat there speechless as tears roll down her cheeks. She knew that Mykal was right. His line of work was just too dangerous, and from the events that transpired tonight, deadly as well. She was only twenty-three years old and had her entire life ahead of her.

"Baby, please promise me that you will leave Miami and make another life for yourself. Something better. I don't know how long I have in this world, only the man upstairs knows that, but I do know that tonight issues must be dealt with, and quickly. Now that my enemy has seen you, you are not safe. And I still don't know who is behind it. I have made a lot of enemies aligning myself with my new partner, and vengeance is always the game. I love you. Always remember that."

Mykal then kissed Alani softly on the forehead, as he had done numerous times before, but this time it was different. This time she knew she would never see him again.

After Mykal left, Alani fell to her knees crying out and thanking God for sparing their lives tonight. While praying, her grandmother's words came back to mind. "Child, if you don't know anything else in the bible, always know the twenty-third Psalms."

At that moment Alani began to recite the Psalm of David over and over again.

A week later, Alani informed her family of her decision to join the military. Of course, no one believed her because Alani was not the typical soldier type. But after constant prayer and affirmation, she knew leaving home was the best thing for her. After a huge argument with her mother, she went to find the nearest army recruiting station, and asked the recruiter, "How soon can I sign up and leave?"

The man in the green uniform looked at her peculiarly and answered, "If you pass the written and physical fitness tests we can have you out of here by the end of next month.

"That's great," Alani responded. "I would like to get as far from Miami as possible."

"Okay ma'am. Would Europe be far enough for you?"

By the end of September, Alani was off to begin her new life as an army soldier.

CHAPTER 9
Feeling Divided

"Hey Darius, this is Jashon. What are you up to this Friday night?"

"Nothing man, just trying to catch up on some sleep from a long week of working."

"Yeah, I hear that, man. Look, me and some of the fellows are heading out to that new club off thirty-eighth street. Just checking to see if you wanted to ride out with us?"

"Yeah, man, that's cool. Come by and scoop me up around ten."

"All right bro, I'll see you then."

Darius knew that whenever Jashon stepped out to a club, he only had one thing on his mind, and that was to hook up with some new lady. Jashon and Darius had been friends for over fifteen years. Symone really didn't care for Jashon. She would tell Darius that his friend switched females like his underwear. Whenever Jashon came to visit Darius, he always had a new woman on his arm. Symone knew that she couldn't control who Darius hung around with, but she did prefer that they would surround themselves with married couples who understood the hardships and turmoil of marriage. Jashon, in her eyes, was another way for Darius to crave and desire the single life.

Darius didn't feel like clubbing tonight, but what else could he do? He felt lonely without his family, and his wife was no longer there to come home to. Who knows, maybe he would meet someone tonight who captured his attention. He no longer had a wife. Darius thought starting a new relationship might not be too bad, for he had needs, too.

CHAPTER 10

The Healing Process

It was a Sunday morning just like any other Sunday. Symone and Jordan had to rush out of the house to make Youth Class and Women's Empowerment, which started at 8:15 a.m. Symone was so glad she'd joined the women's class at church. Originally, she'd had a lot of doubts but after attending the discipleship class and graduating, she knew that she had to keep going. Both classes were really helping her through the depression, divorce proceedings, and Darius's infidelity.

But most important, she was learning how to depend on Jesus like never before. Symone had always believed that God sent people into your life for a lesson, a reason, or a season. And her newfound friendship with Lynn had come during the hardest season of her life.

Lynn, indeed, was a gift from God. The women had befriended each other in church, but also their sons attended basketball camp together. Lynn was the one who convinced Symone to join the discipleship class at the church. Symone felt in her heart that she was not in a place to lead people to Christ. Not during her trials and tribulations. But Lynn reassured her that by taking the course, it would help her find her strength, joy, and peace. But more important, it would draw her closer to the Father.

After attending empowerment classes each Sunday morning and listening to the other women's stories, Symone found herself getting stronger and losing the anger that was within. She learned that Jesus had already forgiven her for her sins, but now was the time for her to forgive herself and Darius. She knew it was going to be hard, but it was possible. If she wanted to be free, she had to learn to forgive.

Lynn, a divorced mother, shared with Symone her marital heartbreak, and how her husband left her and their kids with nothing. Symone realized that she and Lynn had a lot in common. Symone knew that Lynn, indeed, was a lover of Christ, and she shared that love with whomever she encountered. Lynn came to Symone's rescue when her vehicle was repossessed and when there was no food in the house for her and Jordan. Symone often referred to her as a God send whom God sent to help her and encourage her on this new path, And that was exactly what Lynn did. Encouraged her to keep going...

Each empowerment class taught Symone to take back her power, strength, and joy that the enemy had tried to steal. But the class also taught her to take back her mind that he'd tried to destroy, and to let God rebuild and design her into what he'd created her to be. For God did not give her the spirit of fear, but of power. Each class reassured her that God had a bigger plan for her life, but she had to walk in his will and not hers any longer.

Symone was asked to teach a lesson from one of the books the women were currently studying, *Get Unstuck, be Unstoppable* by Valorie Burton. Of course, she was nervous because she had never gotten in front of these women before. After praying over her topic, she asked God to give her the words to say, and to continue to heal her at the same time. Each chapter made her reflect on her own life and how to overcome the hurdles of life. Not only overcome them, but to become unstoppable at the same time. Symone learned to stand on the promises of God during this time, also she learned she had to believe the promises that He made to her. "For I will never leave you, nor forsake you" (Hebrews 13:5). Symone asked God to give her the words to say, so she could go before these women, and please Him, as well.

That night the Holy Spirit told her to speak from her heart. After class, several women commended Symone for sharing her testimony, and some stated that her testimony had helped them, as well. At this moment, she could only hope and pray that God was pleased.

After church service, Symone and some of the ladies decided to go out to eat. Once settled in the restaurant, all the ladies gave thanks that they were being utilized for the Kingdom of God. Not only did each woman have a story of triumph, whether it was a divorce, broken relationship, drug abuse, or health issues, they also encouraged one another and listened as each one reminisced on how God made a way for them at their loneliest point.

Symone knew if Darius could only reach out to the men's ministry group, he could have had this same type of support system. But instead, he looked to the streets and every naysayer who would listen but didn't have his best interests, nor his hurting marriage, at heart.

"Symone honey, are you okay?" asked Lynn.

"Yeah, I'm okay, Lynn."

"Sweetie, you can't continue to dwell on what could've, would've, and should've been, concerning your marriage. We are conquers in Christ Jesus."

"Amen," all the ladies said in unison.

After having lunch, all the ladies hugged one another and departed to their designated areas. Symone felt drained and couldn't wait to get home and relax. Jordan was with the young men's ministry group and they were bringing him home later that evening. After she entered her home and kicked her shoes off by the door, she went to relax in her sunroom downstairs. Once relaxed, she closed her eyes and gave thanks to God for letting her see another day.

"Oh, Mighty God, how wonderful and marvelous is your name. Thank You for loving me, blessing me, and protecting me from harm."

CHAPTER 11
Soldier Up

Alani didn't know what to expect during boot camp. Her stomach was doing flips ever since the plane landed in Ft. Leonard Wood, Missouri. Several of the passengers on the plane were new recruits for the U.S. Army, and each one had a look of terror on their face. No one knew what was ahead of them. All of them had left home for a reason, with hopes for another life for themselves.

After departing the terminal, there stood three army sergeants, standing strong and proud in their green uniforms to welcome the recruits. Once all the recruits gathered their luggage, they were to meet the sergeants outside for roll call. The drive to basic training camp took forever. No one said anything, including the sergeants. Alani just hoped and prayed she was making the right decision.

Once everyone departed the bus, the sergeants went into full army mode. They started screaming and yelling for all recruits to gather their belongings and line up quickly. The poor cadets scrambled to find their places, carrying duffle bags, suitcases, and large sports bags.

Alani got so confused and nervous that she dropped one of her suitcases on a drill sergeant's foot.

Instantly, the female sergeant started to scream out in agony. "Are you crazy, cadet? Do you know who I am?"

Alani stopped in her tracks, trying to hold back her tears. "I'm sorry ma'am," she said in a trembling voice.

"Ma'am! Who are you calling Mam? Do I look like your mother, or even your Grandmother, private?" yelled the female drill sergeant.

At this moment, Alani knew all eyes were on her. She heard the other four drill sergeants snickering behind her back, for all the other cadets to see. Alani couldn't control the tears anymore, and they started to flow down her face uncontrollably.

"Oh, no!" yelled another sergeant. "I think we have a crybaby on our hands."

At this moment, Alani wished she could just dissipate into thin air. "I wish I was home."

CHAPTER 12
Welcome to the Military

After that horrific and embarrassing scene, Alani and the other cadets were told to hustle to their barracks. There they would find their room assignment on the door. At this point, all the cadets were dreadfully tired. Before turning in for the night, the drill sergeants had the cadets run one mile with their luggage in tow.

The tired, staggering new cadets grumbled and moaned, but the drill sergeants continued to laugh and chastise them in an unwelcoming and ruthless manner.

Alani did the best she could during the run. Thank goodness it wasn't a fast pace, but it sure seemed unethical. Some cadets struggled with two or three bags. Many newbies threw their excessive items away just so they could lower their weight and run a little lighter, including Alani. All cosmetics, games, and electronic devices had to go. Either they were confiscated by the drill sergeants, or the recruits had a choice to throw them away.

Upon returning to the barracks, the cadets were informed that the room rooster had been posted. Males were on the first and second floors, and females were on the third and fourth. Wake up was at 4:00 a.m. every morning. Sundays were optional. They could sleep in until 6:00 a.m. Church services began at 7:00 a.m. if they chose to attend church services. However, everyday duties still had to be performed, such as sweeping, mopping, cleaning the bathrooms, buffing and waxing the barrack floors, and of course kitchen duties in the mess hall. Which included peeling potatoes, washing dishes, or slicing fruit, which was for over sixteen-hundred recruits daily.

Many cadets decided they would attend church services. It didn't matter what denomination they were. Two hours away from barracks duties sounded rewarding. Several cadets thought by going to church services they would be able to catch up on some sleep, but little did they know new recruits were always under the scope.

Alani started to feel somewhat homesick and confused about her decision to join the army. She knew she needed clarity, direction, and inner peace, and the only place she could find it was in the Lord's house. It didn't matter if she was in a Protestant church or a Baptist one. There was one thing her grandmother taught her, as a child of the living God, you were never alone. There might come a time when you feel lonely, but you were never alone.

Alani closed her eyes and thanked God for loving her in spite of herself, and in spite of what others said. She was loved. On the way back from the service, she felt at ease. The sermon was "God's Love for His Children." She thought to herself, *No matter what I've done or who I have been with, one thing for certain was God's love for me. But I had to accept Him fully and repent wholeheartedly so that I could abide in His love freely. The type of love God showed his children should never be taken for granted.*

Then Alani started to reflect on one of her favorite bible verses. "I can do all things through Christ who strengthens me" (Philippians 4:13). She knew then that she had made the right decision, and all she had to do was believe in herself, work hard, and watch God do the rest.

Her mind then drifted to Mykal. "Lord, please watch over him and show him your plans for his life. He is a lost sheep and needs his shepherd, like so many of us do. We need your son, Jesus Christ."

CHAPTER 13
He Proposed!

As Symone finished up with morning prayer and meditation in the sunroom, she couldn't help remembering everything that had transpired in her life over the last thirteen years. You see, Symone and Darius's love affair was far from happily ever after. After moving into Darius's home, Symone felt somewhat reluctant, because he had purchased the home during his previous marriage. But to be in alignment with God and the sacrament of marriage, she decided to reside under one roof with her husband in his home, and rent hers out. The move wasn't easy for Symone and Jordan, but Darius continuously reassured her that his home was now their home, and she could remodel and decorate as she liked. It didn't matter to him, because he was glad to have his family under one roof. Darius had two children from his previous marriage: Damisha and Dyon, identical twins and now twenty-one years old. The children had been in Symone's life for nearly twelve years now, ever since they were nine years old.

Symone remembered the first time she met them. It was extremely unsociable. She cooked a dinner at her house for the kids, but when they arrived they both were stand-offish. Each time they visited, she started to feel uncomfortable in her own home. Dyon would speak and was well-behaved, but Damisha would suck her teeth and roll her eyes. Symone and Darius started to realize that his daughter was basically reporting everything back to their mom, Tonia. Whether they had decided to go out to a restaurant, the park, or just shopping, every move they made she would know. Quite often when they got ready to sit down and eat, Tonia would call Darius and tell him to bring her kids home. The worst thing was when the children were with Darius, Tonia would call at least twenty times a day. This type of behavior brought friction between Darius and Symone. How could she ever expect to develop a relationship with his children if she was being constantly blocked by their mother and grandmother? Symone came to feel that if Damisha came to her home only to be an investigator, then she would not be welcome anymore. Eventually, Darius stopped bringing his kids to Symone's home, and she was perfectly okay with that.

As Symone and Darius's relationship deepened, the more issues he started to have with his ex-wife. Tonia. It got so bad that she wouldn't allow Darius to see his children. Symone's heart sank for Darius, because he really missed seeing his children. But he knew that things wouldn't be that way forever. So, Darius and Symone focused on raising Jordan to be the best young man that he could be, with two loving, devoted parents raising him together.

Over the next couple of years Symone and Darius's relationship continued to have its ups and downs, but through it all they survived, and eventually Darius had finally proposed to Symone.

It indeed was a beautiful and mesmerizing night. After dropping Jordan off to his grandmother Suzette, Darius and Symone drove to a remote island in the Florida Keys. After checking into the hotel, they both showered together and made hot passionate love numerous times, then they hit the night life. After a romantic dinner by moonlight, Symone and Darius took a stroll around the island. After stopping at a statue and reading an inscription, Darius professed his love to Symone. Then he kneeled before her and asked if she would spend the rest of her life with him. At that moment, Symone knew that their love could survive anything that life threw their way. But little did she know that their love would be tested beyond the imaginable.

CHAPTER 14
A Ram in the Bush

After their four o'clock wake up and the strenuous tiresome exercise that morning, Alani began to enjoy basic training. She came to realize that this was a mental game and the army would try their best to break you down just to rebuild you as a soldier for wartime situations. Alani started to feel comfortable. Surprising enough, she began to transform physically and mentally. While in training, each cadet learned how to depend on the other to survive and successfully pass the physical fitness training, obstacle course and the shooting range. If any newbie wanted to graduate from basic training and join the army officially, they all needed one another, and that was what drove their teamwork.

Time had literally flown by, and Alani was now in her eighth week of basic training. There were only two weeks left. Now was the time either you passed and went to A.I.T (Advanced Individual Training) or went back home. Alani was determined to pass all requirements, but her only problem was her run time. She had to run two miles in sixteen minutes forty-five seconds, and she could not make that time no matter how hard she tried. She began to feel depressed. There were some cadets who were stronger in certain areas of physical fitness while others weren't strong at all. All cadets insisted on helping each other successfully pass this last requirement which was the most important. But many cadets started to lose hope because the more they tried, the more they felt failure knocking at their door.

Alani started to accept the fact that she would not meet her required time, and found herself crying and praying night after night. "Lord please help me, I've come too far to fail. I do not want to go back home to Miami and look my family in the eye."

But this wasn't about her family, it was about something she had to prove to herself. Sunday morning had come and Alani went to chapel services. The chaplain's sermon was "On Overcoming Your Fears" from the book of Isaiah. "When you pass through the waters, I will be with you; and when you pass through the rivers, they will not sweep over you (Isaiah 43:2).

Alani wanted so much to believe that God would not abandon her when she needed him the most, with the passing of this P.T. test.

After church service, Alani decided to call her dad to confide in him about her fears and struggles. Alani and her dad had just started to mend their relationship prior to her leaving for boot camp.

Dwayne was a recovering alcoholic. As a child Alani could remember her dad always drinking. That was one of the reasons why Alani distant herself from her dad as a teenager and a young adult. After having a breakdown, Dwayne came to realize how much alcohol had destroyed his life and that it would continue to destroy him if he didn't make a change. The day she left for basic training, her dad woke up early to prepare a big breakfast for them both. The two sat there enjoying stewed Bahamian fish with grits along with freshly brewed coffee. Dwayne and Alani had their very first real father and daughter talk. And that was when he promised his daughter that he would never touch alcohol again, and for the very first time in her life she believed him.

"Hey Daddy, how are you?"

"Oh, hey sugar. How is it going army girl?"

"It's okay, Daddy."

"What's wrong Alani? I can hear it in your voice."

"Daddy, I'm scared. The more I try to pass this test, the harder it gets."

"Alani, if you want to come home, then that's what you must do."

"But I don't, Daddy!" Alani cried through the phone.

"Well, if you don't, you have to give it all you got, and I know you can do it, baby girl. You're strong and you're a fighter. Give it your best. Do you hear me?"

"Yes, Daddy, I do. And thank you. I love you, Daddy."

"And I love you too, Alani."

"My turn is up on the phone. I will call you next week, okay? Bye."

Alani felt so much better after speaking to her dad. Although he wasn't around a lot while she grew up, he understood her a lot better than most.

Monday morning had come, and Alani's stomach was in knots. This was her final attempt at passing the P.T test. As she and the other cadets exited the barracks, each one had a look of fear on their face. Alani had continued to pray all the way to the track.

"All right you baby cadets," yelled Drill Sergeant Wright through the bullhorn. "You all have come a long way from being scumbags, and I must say that I am proud of all of you. This is your final attempt. Make sure you leave everything you have on the track. There are no second chances. Graduation is next week. Some of you will graduate, while others will return home to their love ones. We all wish you the best of luck, but remember, never give up. Keep going until you hear the whistle blow, or the sergeant say stop."

Alani had two minutes to complete nineteen push-ups and fifty sit-ups, and had to complete a two-mile run in sixteen minutes forty-five seconds.

"When you hear your name called approach the line, and everyone else should face backwards. Remember, do not start until you hear the whistle blow."

Alani breezed through her push-ups, finishing with thirty-two. Next she completed eighty-eight sit-ups, and still had enough energy for more, but she knew the run was next and that was her weakness.

"All right, cadets, you have five minutes to line up for the run, stretch if you have to, and pray if you must. Just make your time! Remember it's eight laps around the track. You will see a clock as you complete your lap, and of course, we will yell your time out to you. All right, let's get ready to line up cadets."

A few minutes later, the horn blew and off they went.

Alani started off strong. If she kept her breathing intact and focus ahead, she could successfully make her time. But around the time Alani completed her seventh lap, she was basically out of breath. It was such a windy day and the wind was working against her. Alani looked at her time. It now read fourteen minutes thirty-five seconds. That was how long it took her to complete seven laps.

Alani started to slow down, and cried out, "Lord please help me! I cannot do this on my own!"

As she continued to force her way around the track, she was completely exhausted. She did not have enough energy to complete the last lap. Then out of nowhere, a chaplain whom she had never met joined her on the track. Perhaps it was the rears in her eyes, or the despair on her face, but no matter what it was, she was grateful he was there.

The stranger asked, "What time do you need to make?"

"Sir, sixteen minutes forty-five is what I must make."

"Okay," replied the kindhearted stranger. "Let's do it, then."

As Alani began to control her breathing, the chaplain began to shout words of encouragement. "You got this. I'm here with you. I won't let you quit! You're going to make it. Believe in the Father Almighty."

Suddenly Alani felt rejuvenated. She was able to grasp her second wind and control her breathing. Alani began to run as if her life depended on it. The closer she got to the clock, the faster she ran.

"Okay, I can do this," whispered Alani.

Alani and the chaplain sprinted to the finish line as fast as they could.

"Sixteen minutes, forty-two seconds!" yelled the drill sergeant.

Alani bent over to catch her breath, fluttering with excitement.

"I made it!"

"Yes, you did," replied the chaplain in a cheerful voice.

"Thank you, sir! Thank you so much!"

"You're welcome, soldier." And then he drifted off into the crowd

Alani never asked him his name. With tears in her eyes and joy in her heart, she looked up toward heaven and whispered, "Thank you, Father, I Thank you!"

Graduation Day had finally arrived. Apart from a few cadets, one hundred thirty-seven graduated from her class. Alani had invited her family, but due to the freezing weather conditions, they could not attend. Alani was okay with that. She was just excited becoming a soldier in the United States Army.

Before she knew it, Alani had completed her twelve weeks of A.I.T (Advanced Individual Training) for her new job as a 92 Alpha, military supply logistics personnel. Those twelve weeks went by very quickly. Then she was off to her first duty station in Germany.

She was ecstatic to be living in another country. Although she was a little nervous, she knew that God was with her no matter where she went. Her new assignment and home for the next two years was Katterbach, Germany, Third Battalion. Since she'd joined ROTC (Reserve Officer Training Course) in high school, she was able to come in with the rank of PFC (Private First Class) which meant she earned a little more money than a private and could advance in rank quickly if she chose. Alani knew that two years was a long time, but she felt it would become an adventure and experience that she would never forget.

CHAPTER 15

Keep your Hands Off

Symone and Darius had started planning their wedding immediately. Symone's family was thrilled that the two had finally decided to unite as one under God's covering. The excitement in Jordan's voice and eyes made everything worthwhile. Jordan constantly repeated to everyone "Were getting married," or 'My wedding." He was more excited about the wedding than his mom and dad.

Mixed feelings reigned in Darius's family, especially Gertrude. But Darius reassured Symone that nothing would spoil their marriage or their new lives together.

Their wedding approached quickly, for September 23rd was the day. The two started to argue more frequently. Maybe it was the pressure of planning the wedding or the pressure from the families, but whatever the reason was, the two started to feel the pressure. Symone and Darius's tempers became shorter with one another. Symone decided that it was best for them to seek outside professional help. They went to seek pastoral counseling for engaged couples, and independent counseling through a marriage therapist.

The more they explained their issues, the more distant they became. Symone's main issues were Darius always referring to his first marriage and his mother's constant meddling in their relationship. Darius complained that Symone should be more understanding regarding his mom, and be patient with his kids. But through it all, Symone knew she loved

Darius and hoped their problems would work themselves out. But unfortunately, things started to take a turn for the worse.

On this particular day, Darius decided to go watch his son Dyon play basketball. Usually he would invite Symone and Jordan to come along, but that night he didn't. Symone asked why they could not attend together.

Darius responded, "Tonia will be there and you two do not get along."

Of course, this bothered Symone, because she didn't care if Tonia was there or not, and it would not have been the first time they were in each other's presence. Darius and Symone argued until Darius stormed out the house. This infuriated Symone. At that point, she started to question herself. Was there something going on between those two? The more she thought about it, the angrier she became. Darius returned home late that night, after midnight. Symone had tried her best to control her temper, but after calling Darius several times that night only to be directed straight to his voicemail, that was not making the matter better, only worse. Symone quietly lay in her bed pretending to be sleep as he went to the bathroom for a quick shower. After leaving the bathroom, Darius kissed Symone goodnight.

Symone asked Darius where he was that late at night and why did he not answer his phone? Darius responded he'd been with his son and didn't hear the phone ring. Symone didn't believe anything he said, and once again they started yelling at one another. Darius insisted nothing was going on between him and Tonia, but Symone didn't know what to believe anymore. All she wanted now was Darius away from her.

Symone went through the house removing all of Darius's clothing, throwing them on the floor and yelling for him to get out of her house. She was so in love with this man and about to marry him, but she couldn't marry someone she didn't trust. Tears started streaming down Symone's face. The feeling of betrayal was just too much. She started to push Darius until he'd had enough, and before she knew it Darius was being transported in an ambulance and she was being arrested for assault. Flashes of Jordan ran across Symone's mind.

"Lord God, what just happened?"

Symone had heard of people snapping, but never would she have imagined that it would happen to her.

CHAPTER 16
Turn -Up

Alani began to enjoy her new life as a soldier. Physical fitness was every morning at 6:00 a.m., rain, snow, sleet, or sunshine. Sometimes they ran three to five miles a day, and others it was another form of physical training. Alani's running endurance became better. She began to enjoy running and the relaxation, freedom, and enjoyment it brought to her life. Slowly, she began to make friends in her new home so far away, and the soldiers started treating each other like family. They helped one another, encouraged one another, ate together, ran together, and partied hard together. On Sundays, a few soldiers, including Alani, began making Sunday dinners for their entire floor. If a soldier couldn't cook or chose not to cook, they would pay their portion and wait for their plate. The third floor was the party spot on the weekends; music would blast from several rooms all at one time and dance competitions were held in the hallway. Some rooms held card games, another might be a dominos room or a movies room, and lastly was the drinking room where soldiers would take shots and have mixed drinks to their heart's content. The community that they established among one another was strong and enduring.

With perseverance and hard work, Alani started to advance in rank. She came in as a PFC (Private First Class, or an E-3) and now she was promoted to a Specialist, or an E-4. An E-4 was treated with a little more respect and was known to be dependable. Alani's family back home in Miami was so proud of her that several gift boxes started to arrive monthly. Her mom Suzette sent her the most, including stuffed animals, especially teddy bears. For some reason, teddy bears always comforted Alani, and her mother knew that.

Alani started to date other soldiers, but never anything too serious. At one point she started to date outside her race, and Alani enjoyed it. She didn't care about the stares or the whispers behind their backs, but as long as he treated her with respect and showered her with gifts, then she was content.

But as hard as she tried, she just could not forget about Mykal. She could only hope and pray that he would not end up shot or even killed in his line of work. So many times, she wanted to pick up the phone to call him, but never got up enough nerve. What would she say to him? Had she honestly forgiven him for the danger he put her in—basically a near death experience? Nevertheless, Alani knew in her heart that Mykal had loved her enough to let her go. If it wasn't for Mykal persuading her to get away and travel the world, she probably would never have joined the army, and no matter what occurred between the two of them, Alani would always be grateful to him for that.

CHAPTER 17

It's A Test!!

Mykal thought of Alani daily, but he couldn't allow his personal feelings for her to distract him from his business. He believed he'd fallen in love with Alani, and he knew deep down in his heart that no other woman had affected him as Alani. She made him see hope in a dark situation, and she believed in him when no one else did. But more important, she was loyal and never took his affection for granted.

Mykal remembered the first time he tested her loyalty. He had invited her over for a candlelit seafood dinner. Both enjoyed seafood, and he'd looked forward to cooking that night. He had stopped doing business early that evening and made the necessary phone calls to let his constituents know that he did not want to be disturbed for the rest of the day. Before Alani arrived, he wanted to make sure to set the trap. In his bedroom he counted out ten thousand dollars, then decided to leave the money on his dresser all scattered. He knew if a single bill had been taken, Alani could not be trusted and he could not keep her in his life.

Mykal looked at the time and realized he had less than an hour to complete dinner, shower, then dress. Mykal decided to cook a garlic lobster scampi tossed with mussels and jumbo shrimp. For the side he decided on a Greek salad with a creamy vinaigrette sauce, and for dessert a sweet almond macaroon tart. To complete their beautiful night together, a rich bottle of chardonnay. Mykal loved to cook; it relaxed him and brought him a sense of peace and reassurance. Mykal shared with Alani that he got his love of cooking from watching the cooking network on TV, but more important, from his grandmother. Mykal use to watch his grandmother cook as a young boy. Everything she made was from scratch, but also from love. Mykal recalled his Grandma Jessie telling him one day, "When you cook, son, you got to put some love in it. That's the key to a good homemade meal."

After finishing preparing the table setting and putting the bottle of wine on ice, Mykal had twenty minutes to shower and change. He rushed to the shower, completed his personal hygiene, and slipped into his linen powder blue short set. Around 8:45 p.m. his doorbell rang, and he knew that it was his lovely date Alani. Mykal opened the door for his guest and there she stood, stunning in a floral silk handkerchief spaghetti-strap dress. Her heels were open-toed with straps that tied to her ankles, and she was wearing her favorite perfume, "Beautiful" by Lorie Elle. Mykal loved that scent on Alani. That was why he had purchased it for her last month.

Alani entered his candlelit home and was very pleased at his décor, but most of all she was excited to be in his presence. The sounds of Kenny G's smooth jazz saturated the entire house. Mykal and Alani enjoyed their delicious dinner by candlelight. Alani couldn't believe what a good cook Mykal was. The conversation was good, as well. They talked about Alani's day at work and where she saw herself in five years. She also talked about returning to school for her bachelor's degree, but she couldn't find the time. Mykal spoke about his childhood and how he loved to cook.

"I am full!" Alani exclaimed.

"Oh no, sweet girl. I cooked a special dessert just for you."

"Oh really?" teased Alani, flirting with her fork. "Already?"

"In time, my beautiful lady, believe me, in time," Mykal whispered back in a devilish tone. "But I am referring to my delicious homemade almond macaroons tarts that I prepared for you tonight."

"Okay, but please give me a few minutes to digest this dinner. I just need a few minutes to rest and freshen up."

"So be it, my lady, the bathroom is down the hall to the right."

Alani excused herself from the table and went to recheck her hair and make-up in the bathroom. "Girl you look good!" She smirked as she complimented herself in the mirror.

After returning to the dining area she couldn't help but smile at how Mykal's eyes were fixated on her as she entered. She could see him blushing from ear to ear.

"Now, didn't I tell you that you looked stunning tonight?"

"Not that I can recall, but I will forgive you anyway.""

My dear lady, I'm getting aroused just by you being in my presence and I want desperately to taste you...but let's enjoy the rest of our evening."

The macaroon almond tart was absolutely delicious.

"Oh, a man that can cook like this and clean! I believe I just struck gold," Alani teased Mykal.

Both of them laughed loudly. "All right, young lady, I want you to go relax while I tackle these dishes."

"What! You don't use your dishwasher?" Alani questioned.

"Not really. I like to keep my hands soft and clean, and one way is to get manicures, or washing dishes by hand. And my dear, I like to bust those subs occasionally. Plus, it gives me time to think and put things in perspective. Now, go relax your fine self. My home is yours to enjoy. I have a small theater in my room and a large plush king mattress, a jacuzzi tub, and a weight room in the back, so the choice is yours. Oh, I forgot, Snowflake is in the back sleeping."

"Who?" Alani asked. My three-year-old pit bull. She's quiet, but if you wake her she can be quite difficult."

"Don't worry, I'll pass," Alani replied.

Alani proceeded to walk through the house until she got to Mykal's bedroom. Spread across his king-sized plush mattress was a red silk kimono with a dozen red roses. Lying next to the flowers was an envelope. She opened the envelope and read the card. Instantly her body started to tingle all over, but also her inner womanhood started to drip with moisture. Alani became so mesmerized by Mykal's show of affection that she almost missed the astonishing amount of money that was scattered all over his dresser. Alani wasn't sure what to make of it, but suddenly she remembered a conversation with her cousin Nyisha awhile back.

"Ballers will sometimes set a trap to see who they can and cannot trust in their circle."

"Good try, Mykal, but I'll pass." Alani decided to find a movie and relax in the so soft and comfortable down comforter on the king-sized bed.

Mykal had finished washing the dishes and cleaning the kitchen. He really like having Alani in his life, but he knew not everyone was trustworthy, especially in his line of work. Deep in his heart he hoped that Alani had not touched any of the cash. Mykal walked down the hall into his room only to find Alani curled up asleep next to her gifts. He smiled instantly and thought to himself, *She is even beautiful in her sleep.* Mykal looked over at the dresser. All the money looked to be right where he'd left it. With a sense of relief, Mykal took the money into the next bedroom and counted it to be certain. After he finished counting, he still had ten thousand dollars. Feeling rejuvenated, Mykal returned to his bedroom and snuggled tightly beside Alani. He kissed her sweetly on the forehead, then he drifted off to sleep.

CHAPTER 18

Snapped

Symone was booked and charged with assault and battery. In her mind she knew that this had been someone else. No way would she have allowed someone to drive her to a point of no return. After taking her mugshot, she was granted one phone call. She called Michelle, who had Jordan that night, and explained to her what had transpired between her and Darius. Symone asked Michelle to contact her family as soon as possible. Michelle reassured Symone that everything would be okay, and she would look after Jordan until Symone or her family arrived.

Symone then thought about Darius. "Lord, please keep him safe. I'm so sorry for what I did. I didn't mean to." Symone did not recognize that other person. It was as if she was overcome by anger, almost like stepping out of herself. Symone couldn't believe that Darius had actually put his hands on her. But to make matters worse, he dragged her through her very own house by her hair, kicking and screaming. After that, Symone had snapped.

"Why did he do that to me, God? Why?"

Symone always remembered her grandmother words. "Never allow a man to hit you or beat you, but if he does you better fight with everything in you, then get away."

Symone sat in jail for two days. She refused to eat or mingle with the other inmates. All she wanted to do was sleep and pray. Symone's mom, sisters, and aunt had driven up from Miami immediately once they received the phone call from Michelle informing them of what had taken place. Michelle spoke to Suzette, Symone's mom, letting her know that she had Jordan and he was okay, but he was crying for his mother. Once she spoke to Symone's family, Michelle called the hospital to check on Darius. She found out that he had a flesh wound and had received a few stitches, but he was fine and released from the hospital two hours ago.

Suzette swung into action, searching for a lawyer in Savannah to represent her daughter. Her heart ached for her daughter, and she knew she had to get her out of there quickly. Suzette found out through Michelle that once Darius was released from the hospital, he came by to pick up Jordan from her house. She'd tried to talk Darius out of it, but he wanted his son. Once Suzette received that information, she knew that time was of the essence. Suzette was furious that Darius would endanger her daughter like this. She knew that they were having issues, but my God, nothing like this. Symone's sister Lisette, along with their mother and Aunt Casey decided to drive together to be there when Symone went before the court. Phoenix, her other sister, decided to meet them at the courthouse. Everyone was scared for Symone, but they were all a praying family who believed in the miracles of Jesus Christ. And that's what they needed now, for God to intervene in this horrible situation.

Monday morning came, and Symone appeared before the judge via satellite wearing an orange jumpsuit issued by the correction facility. Sitting in the courtroom were her family and Darius. Symone felt humiliated and ashamed. Here she was, fighting against domestic violence, and now she and Darius had become part of the problem. The look of empathy showed on her family's faces. Symone saw the tears in her mother's and her sister's eyes. She was informed that the judge was stern and wasn't too big on leniency, but like her lawyer told her, she had never been in trouble with the court, and she was a veteran. But it couldn't hurt to pray for favor. Symone couldn't believe that Darius spoke on her behalf. He also informed the judge that both of them were wrong, and that Jordon needed his mother. Cynthia, Symone's lawyer, agreed but also reminded the judge that Symone actions were due to Darius physically assaulting her client first. The judge granted bail for Symone and that she would be placed on probation for one year.

After being processed out of the correction facility, Symone was released. She saw her family outside waiting for her. Immediately she ran into her mother's arms and cried her heart out. Suzette held her daughter as tightly as she possibly could, reassuring her that everything would be all right.

"Momma," Symone whimpered faintly, drenched with tears, "Where is my son?"

CHAPTER 19
Shedding of Tears

Darius had just left the courthouse and the bonding office. He knew in his heart that he helped contribute to the pain and anguish that Symone and her family were feeling. After picking Jordan up from Michelle's house, he reassured his son that his mommy would be back soon. All weekend Jordan had cried for his mom, but Darius couldn't give his son a direct answer.

That night he fell on his knees, crying for God to forgive him for what he had done to his son, but most important, to the woman he loved.

CHAPTER 20
Fight Another Day

Symone felt so happy to be back home. After taking a long, hot shower and eating a decent meal, she just wanted to lie down. Symone went into her closet and prayed, thanking God for bringing her home and keeping her during that dreadful time in her life. After getting up, she went to climb in her bed. There Symone dozed off, only to be woken up hours later. At first, she thought she was dreaming, but once she felt his hand on her face and heard his voice saying "Mommy! Mommy!" she knew it was real.

Symone grabbed her son and held him tightly, crying and whispering, "I've missed you so much!"

"But Mommy, I cried for you. Where were you?"

"I know, honey, and Mommy is so sorry that I hurt you or made you cry. But know that Mommy loves you more than anything, and will never leave you again."

Symone's family stayed with her and Jordan for a few days. Suzette didn't want to leave her daughter just yet, but she had to get back to work. Her sisters Lizzie and Phoneix also had to leave, yet she was so happy that they came to support her and take care of Jordan during this difficult time. Before everyone departed to their destinations, they gathered for prayer and singing. They all kissed one another and reassured Symone to stay encouraged, and to keep close to God because He was the only one that could bring her through. Then Symone and Jordan were left by themselves. As part of the probation, she was not to have any communication with Darius for one year. Visitations between him and Jordan had to be through a third party.

For the next few days, Symone felt like a zombie. She was raised in church all her life, but now she felt that God was angry with her, and that He had turned his back on her. Symone basically slept all day. She thought she could sleep away the pain. In actuality, sleep was the only thing that brought her peace. Day after day she got up fixed Jordan breakfast, turned on the TV for him, and went back to sleep.

But on one particular morning, Symone woke up in a dark place. she began to question, was she a good person? How could she allow anyone to drive her to a place of no return? *How could my reaction hurt Darius, the man I love? Lord, my son deserves a better mother than me.* Guilt and a feeling of shame started to take over Symone's life. She couldn't stop hating herself, and she knew there was only one way to stop it. Symone went into her kitchen, grabbed the sharpest knife that she could find, and went back into her bedroom. She knew that her mom would take good care of Jordan. At this point she felt she couldn't give him what he needed.

Symone picked up the phone and called her cousin Ashlee, who lived not too far from her. Ashlee picked up almost instantly. Symone asked if she could call her sister Phoenix to come pick Jordan up. Ashlee heard the tears in Symone's voice, and asked why. Symone then confided that she couldn't do it anymore, and that Jordan deserves a better mother than her. Symone knew by taking her own life the pain and embarrassment she caused herself and others would be no more. Ashlee pleaded with Symone to think about Jordan and what this would do to him. Ashlee admitted that she, herself, had tried to commit suicide about three years ago. She then went into detail about how she had taken an entire bottle of anti-depressants and drank a fifth of vodka behind it. She admitted that it was only by the grace of God that her mom had decided to stop by that night.

"I didn't know I was laid out unconscious, Symone. After my mom walked in and discovered what I was trying to do, she immediately called the ambulance and they rushed me to the hospital and pumped my stomach. I woke up two days later in a hospital bed, surrounded by my parents and four children. Symone, I've been there. I never told anyone what happened to me because I was ashamed and so tired. Tired of crying, and feeling stuck in a life that I didn't recognize anymore. Symone, I was so depressed Satan tried to take me out. After Kevin left us, I didn't know how I was going to make it without him. Taking care of the kids with no support from him, I became stressed and lost at the same time, worrying about how I was going to feed me and my children. But God said, 'No!' So, my dear I'm here to tell you, you're going to make it, too. Fall on your knees and ask God to forgive you, and lead you down the right path. But most important, you must ask that the Father grant you the strength and courage to fight another day. You cannot do this on your own. This is far bigger than you and me. We know how much you and Darius love each other, but now it's about Jordan, and he needs his mother to fight for her life and for his, too. Get up, Symone, and fight for your freedom, happiness, and your destiny. This shall not end the way you want it to end, but how God wants it to end. Now you, go take a long, hot shower, put on some clothes and comb your hair. But whatever you do, don't stop moving. I must go get the kids now, but I will call to check on you later. I love you, Symone, and I promise you things will get better. Trust God through this pain. He is there."

Symone couldn't believe that Ashlee tried to commit suicide. She always seemed so happy.

Then out of nowhere, Jordan ran into his mother's room and jumped into her bed. "Mommy I love you," he called out, then left just as quickly as he'd appeared.

Symone dropped to her knees in prayer, seeking God in all this confusion and pain. With tears streaming down her face, she asked God for help. "Jesus, I need you, please forgive me for what I was about to do. I beg of you, do not turn your back on me. Right now, I feel that you are so far away, and I feel that I let you down. I know I let my family down, but most important, I let myself down. One thing I do know is that you are real, and that the devil would love to take me out. According to your word, 'The thief cometh not, but to steal, kill and destroy, but you come that I might have life more abundantly' (John 10:10). So, my prayer today is that you give me the strength I need to keep going. A new life in you and please save me from myself. In Jesus name I pray. Amen."

CHAPTER 21
Oh!! Master Sergeant

Before Alani knew it, a whole year had gone by, and now she was starting on her second tour in Germany. Alani and several of her friends began to travel all throughout Europe. One weekend they visited Amsterdam, and the next weekend was Paris. It was so much fun traveling abroad and learning about other cultures. Alani was excited and proud of herself that she had earned the rank of sergeant in the United States Army within three years. Recently she had started dating a senior ranking sergeant, Brexton Nyles. Master Sergeant Nyles was ten years older than Alani, but one of the things Alani admired about him was his professionalism and his poise. Sometimes MSG Nyles would flirt with Alani and show her favoritism. He began to shower her with gifts and displayed a lot of affection. Brexton lived off base, so Alani started spending a lot of time at his apartment. Initially, Alani was not attracted to Brexton, but with his rank and status, eventually she started to develop real feelings for him. Months had passed, and she found herself falling for him. Brexton confessed to Alani that he and his wife were currently separated, and he did not see them ever reconciling. Alani knew it was wrong to be with a married man, but she knew that Brexton loved her deeply, and that was what kept their fire alive.

Little by little, Alani started to see a change in Brexton. He started to become a little controlling of where she went, what she wore, and whom she was hanging around with. She wanted to keep Brexton happy and their relationship secure, so she stopped going out altogether with her friends and spent the rest of her tour with Brexton. The time had come for Alani to leave Germany. Her next assignment was Ft. Bragg in North Carolina. Alani had known that her assignment in Germany was not permanent, but Brexton had become a significant part of her life and she did not want to lose him, not when she had finally found love again.

Two weeks later, Alani was finally processed into Fort Bragg 82nd Airborne Division. The transition went smoothly. Now that she was a sergeant in the U.S. Army, Alani was authorized BHA, a basic housing allowance that permitted her to live off base in her very own apartment. Alani settled into a cozy two-bedroom apartment which included a washer and dryer and a balcony view. She was overjoyed that she had her very own place that she could decorate as she liked. Alani began her new journey as an Airborne soldier. Brexton and Alani spoke every day, but it was hard for her not to be with him. He had become part of her life. Brexton constantly reminded Alani how much he loved her and reassured her that they would be back together again.

Nearly two months later, around midnight, Alani was awoken by a drastic pounding at her front door. She immediately became frightened, and didn't know what to do. She knew her friends would call before they came over. Who could this be? Alani retrieved the heavy wooden stick that her grandmother gave to her when she went home. "A pretty girl like you should always protect herself. Baby, always keep it in your home. You never know, not everybody's got good sense." Alani had that wooden stick in her right hand and her phone in her left, ready to dial 911.

She approached the door and asked, "Who is it?"

"Baby its me!"

Alani knew she must have been hallucinating, for she thought she heard Brexton's voice. "Excuse me?" she replied.

"Alani, it's me, Brexton."

CHAPTER 22

Change the Clock

Darius was healing quite quickly. He couldn't believe what had transpired between him and Symone. He loved her very much and couldn't understand why they argued like they did. He knew with his excessive baggage—an ex-wife who constantly meddled in their relationship, his children who constantly disrespected Symone, and his mother who continued to speak negative about their relationship—were a lot for her. But he reassured her that things wouldn't always be that way. Darius knew that a lot of this was brought on by him, but he just wanted to keep everyone happy.

A week prior to this, he and Symone had another outburst. An old girlfriend of Darius had reached out to him about a kiss they once shared, and she confessed how much she missed him. After reading the text on his phone, Symone became heated. She went into the kitchen, picked up a large pot and filled it with ice and cold water, then proceeded to the sofa where Darius was sleeping and threw the ice water all over him. For a moment Darius thought he was drowning in the ocean. He started yelling at the top of his lungs.

"Oh, sorry sweetheart. I thought you needed to cool off."

Darius knew that Symone had trust issues from her previous relationship, and he wanted to reassure her that he only wanted her. He started reflecting on what he could have done differently. *Maybe I should have called Symone to let her know how long I was going to be, but what upset Symone the most was that he did not invite her or their son to the game. If only they* could relive that horrific evening. But he knew he could not erase the past, only to learn from it. Would they ever get past this? *How would this effect Jordan and our families?* he wondered.

Day by day, Symone grew stronger and things got a little easier. She found herself laughing and smiling again. Her prayer life increased as did her worshipping. Not only did she worship at church, but Symone started to worship in her own house. She began to seek God in everything she did. Symone began to remember the bible scripture, "For I know the plans I have for you declares the Lord, plans to prosper you and not to harm you, plans to give you hope and a future" (Jeremiah 29:11 NIV). She also began to meditate and recite (Psalms 143:8-12) every day. She repeated it until she memorized it. Through all the heartache, pain, and courts, Symone and Darius somehow found their way back to each other. Through all her praying and fasting, she felt that God had given them another chance. And most important, she learned how to forgive herself and Darius. She could only hope that Darius had forgiven her, too.

CHAPTER 23
Wedding Day

A year later, Darius and Symone stood in front of their pastor, family and friends to unite under God's covenant of marriage. This, indeed, had to be one of the best days of Symone's life. Her mother, sisters, and best friend were right by her side all the way, but she believed that Jordan was the most excited. As she walked down the aisle, arms joined with her father's, she couldn't believe that she and Darius had made their way back to each other. As she walked down the aisle, tears emerged from her eyes. She continually gazed into Darius eyes as the piano played. At this moment, nothing else mattered. She was his and he was hers. She noticed the dirty looks that were coming from Darius's mom Gertrude and his daughter Damisha, but that didn't matter. Destiny had finally spoken, and God was now combining the two bodies into one in holy matrimony.

Symone was so very happy, and for a while everything was good for them both. It felt so good living under one roof with her husband, to fall asleep in his arms and wake up together was all she'd dreamt of. Symone began to decorate the house as if it were her own home, but deep down it never felt like home, no matter how hard she tried. Darius began to accompany Symone and Jordan to Sunday service every other Sunday, and it felt so good. Symone would peek out the corner of her eye to see Darius clapping his hands or singing with the worship team. It gave her a sense of pride that her husband had become affiliated with the church. Now what she desired was that Darius accept Jesus Christ as his personal savior and be baptized and saved. But with constant prayer, it would eventually happen.

The first year of their marriage was wonderful. Everyone was happy, especially Jordan. But the next year started to get rocky. Symone knew that all marriages had their issues, but she and Darius started arguing more frequently than ever. It got so bad that he stopped praying and attending service with Symone and Jordan altogether. After an argument, Darius would leave the house for three full days. Symone would constantly worry and pray that whatever was happening between them, God would come and intervene. If not, how would they make it?

CHAPTER 24

Negative Spirits

Gertrude had come to visit Darius and his children. Symone knew now that whenever Gertrude visited, Darius's attitude toward her would change. Symone couldn't understand how Darius would alienate his very own wife to please his mother, but he did. Darius had assured Symone that she was exaggerating, but she knew better. Gertrude had decided to stay with Darius's ex-wife Tonia and his children. Honestly, it was perfectly okay with Symone. Symone laughed at how Gertrude used to speak so negatively of Tonia, and now they had become best friends. Well, to each his own.

Symone soon started to pray over the house that she and Darius shared. She remembered her grandmother and pastor telling her that the best way to keep bad spirits out of your home was to get some anointing oil and pray over everything in the house, including your children and spouse. Darius would look at Symone and laugh, but she believed in prayer and in the Holy Spirit, and she certainly wanted peace and tranquility in their home.

But Symone sensed deep in her spirit that something was coming, and it was not good.

CHAPTER 25

Let Me Introduce Myself

Alani could not believe that Brexton had gotten his military orders changed to be with her. Originally, Brexton was assigned to Ft. Benning, Georgia, but somehow those orders got deleted. Alani and Brexton became inseparable. There were some nights she stayed at his place and others he was at hers. Finally, for the first time in Alani's life, she knew that she was in love with this man and wanted no other. Brexton continued to provide, and spoiled Alani like crazy. In addition, he protected her and loved her, and what more could a girl want? Then Alani remembered that Brexton was not fully hers yet—not until his divorce was final.

Alani had packed her overnight bag to spend the weekend with Brexton. She knew that the issue of his divorce had to be discussed, and tonight would be the night. Alani arrived at Brexton's apartment, but she didn't see his truck in the parking lot, so she let herself in. As soon as she walked in, the aroma of sweet baked apple pie filled the atmosphere. Brexton had left an apple pie in the oven, and on the countertop she saw his note.

Hey baby, I'm going to pick up dinner, I left a pie in the oven to keep warm, please take it out and I'll see you soon, Love Brexton.

Alani was completely drained. Her body was still sore from the brigade's six mile run that morning, then later that afternoon she'd had to counsel two of her soldiers for missing morning formation. All she wanted to do now was relax in a hot bubble bath and receive a fabulous full body massage from Brexton.

As soon as Alani undressed to step into the tub, she heard the phone ring. *If it's important they'll call back*, she said to herself. Just then, she heard Brexton's cell phone ringing from the bedroom. Okay, maybe it was Brexton. Alani stepped out of the tub and rushed to answer the phone "Hey, baby!"

"Excuse me?" the female voice responded from the other end.

Alani felt frozen. *It couldn't be*, she thought.

"I'm calling to speak to my husband, Brexton. Is he available?"

"No, he isn't ma'am," Alani replied very short.

"Ma'am? Girl don't even go there with me! So, you're the one he's playing house with? Sleeping with a married man with three kids."

"Look, Liza. Are you finished?" asked Alani very sternly.

"Oh, well, so you do know who I am?"

"Yes, Liza, I do. And I also know that you guys have been separated for at least four years and the divorce is pending because you won't sign the papers."

"How, young lady, do you know that?"

"Because Brexton and I have been together for over two years and we share everything with each other."

"Is that so?" Liza asked very sarcastically. "Well, my sweet young naïve girl, how long did you say you and Brexton been together?"

"Brexton and I have been together for almost two years now."

"Hmm," Liza said. "Wait, is your name Alani?"

"Yes, it is. How do you know that?"

"Because Brexton told me there was a young girl who constantly sent him notes and continuously flirted with him."

Alania started to laugh so hard that she scared herself. "Lady, stop lying! Brexton told me you were crazy, but now I know."

"Oh, really? Well, let me tell you something, you naïve girl. Your dear sweet Brexton has been lying to both of us. And as far as the divorce goes, he is the one who won't sign the divorce papers. I am perfectly fine divorcing the two-timing lying, bipolar fool. I assume you haven't seen the other side of Brexton? Well, let me break it down for you. He becomes extremely controlling, violent, and completely vulgar. Let me ask you this. Has he started dictating who your friends are or what you can wear? Oh, better yet, does he want you to spend all of your time with him? Well, from your quietness I suspect he has. Soon, sweetheart, you will see the real Brexton Nyles, and I mean the dark, ugly side."

"Well, if he is all that bad and bipolar as you claim he is, then why haven't you left him?"

"Not that it's any of your business, but I've been married to this man for over seventeen years, through heartache, pain, and his extramarital affairs. As crazy as it is, I still love the fool. Honestly, do you think you're the only side piece he has had throughout the years? I must say he has been with you for the longest, so maybe he thinks he's in love with you. Maybe he is, but it doesn't matter anymore. He retires soon, and I am entitled to half, and once that's done, he's all yours!"

Just when Alani was about to respond, she heard Brexton coming in, "Look, Liza this has been quite entertaining, but I have to go." Angrily, Alani slammed the phone down, fuming at what had just transpired.

"Alani, what's wrong?" Brexton asked after setting the food down own on the counter. "Who was that on the phone?"

"Your wife, Brexton! Your wife!" Alani screamed with tears in her eyes.

CHAPTER 26
Grow Up Already!

Darius walked around the house in silence. He maintained his distance from Symone and Jordan. Symone continued to cook dinner and ignore his childish behavior, but she knew he was not happy with her and her relationship with his mother. Later that night, Darius chose to eat by himself in the bedroom. After cleaning the kitchen and getting Jordan ready for bed, Symone entered their bedroom feeling as if she was walking on pins and needles.

"Honey, please talk to me," she pleaded with Darius.

"Symone, my mom doesn't feel comfortable in our home, and you're the only one that can make it right."

"Okay, Darius. what do you want me to do?"

"I need you to apologize to her."

"Excuse me? If anyone deserves an apology, it's me, Darius. I have tried to be polite to your mom and all she ever did was disrespect me and talk negatively toward me and our marriage."

"Symone, she hasn't forgiven you for when you cut me."

"Oh, okay, but it's okay for you to drag me through my house by my hair kicking and screaming? What about that Darius? Is that okay?"

"Look, Symone, this is not a debate. Are you going to apologize or not?"

"Hell no! This is our marriage, and I will be so glad when you stop allowing your mother to direct this union. Everything that happens between us, you run and tell your mother. You're the reason why there is so much turmoil between us, Darius. There are days when I feel like I married a little boy instead of a grown man. I have never asked you to choose me over your mom and I never will, but you act like loving and being married to me is a distraction from the relationship that you have with your mother. I didn't make a vow to Gertrude, but to you in front of God and our family and friends. Why can't you see what you're doing to our family, Jordan and me? Darius you're hurting us!"

Symone started to cry. Her heart was breaking and she didn't know what else to do. She loved her husband very much, but the meddling of Gertrude in their marriage was starting to become unbearable. She looked up and saw there were tears in her husband's eyes, as well. She could tell that he was torn between the two women in his life, and honestly, he had no idea what to do, for he was lost himself. Symone decided to go shower before either one of them said something they would later regret.

While standing in the shower with the hot water running against her caramel-colored body, she began to sob wholeheartedly. "Lord help me. What am I to do in this marriage? I'm so tired of fighting with Darius about his mom's interference." She then began to reflect on an article she read last week, "The Consequences of the Lack of Maternal Attachment." After reading the article, she'd develop a better understanding of why Darius behaved the way he did. The article described emotional dependency when it came to men and their mothers. If the mother left their son for a period of time in his adolescent years, the male child would become defensive and protective of their mothers. Later in his adulthood, if his wife or significant other would disappoint him, he would become detached and feel a sense of betrayal, or even a sense of rage. The wife would become the enemy in his mind, and his mother would become his safe haven.

Symone was startled when Darius pulled the shower curtain back. "Baby, I'm sorry. I love you and our family very much, but sometimes I feel I must please everybody—you, my momma, the children, and my family.

"But that's just it, Darius. You can't please everybody. It's impossible. If you keep trying to please everyone, you're going to end up losing yourself and what we fought so hard for. Our marriage is in serious trouble. I mean, you won't even pray with me anymore, and then you stopped going to church with Jordan and me."

"Symone, will you forgive me again for acting crazy?"

"Of course I will, but has got to stop!"

"I hear you, but can I join you in the shower?"

"Yes, you may," she said with a wicked smile on her face.

Darius grabbed onto Symone as if his life depended on it, kissing her from her naval and working his way up to her neck. Then slowly they commenced to making sweet, magical love right there in the shower.

CHAPTER 27
The Talk

The following morning, Darius and Symone apologized to one another, and commenced to praying for one another, their marriage, and their families. After the prayer, Symone asked if there was a positive male figure in his life whom he trusted, that he could confide in. Symone had surrounded herself with goal-oriented prayer warriors, and confiding in them was the best thing she had ever done. Darius didn't have that same support system. He often told her he wished he had. Symone had tried several times to get Darius to join the Men's Empowerment Group at church, or to surround himself with Christian married men who could help him in his walk, but he'd always refused. Darius decided to call Mr. Hollins, an older gentleman whom he had admired and respected for several years, to ask his advice on this matter.

"Good morning, Mr. Hollins. This is Darius. Sorry to call you this early, but I need your opinion on a marital issue that my wife and I were discussing."

"That's okay, Darius. How can I assist you and your beautiful wife this glorious morning?"

"We're good, thank you, sir. My wife feels that by me sharing information with my mom about our marriage, it's causing problems between us, and I feel she's overreacting." Darius went on to tell Mr. Hollins about the argument they'd had last night, and about his mother refusing to stay with them, but stayed with Tonia his ex-wife, instead.

Suddenly, Mr. Hollins interrupted. "Darius, my son, bringing your mother into your marriage is the worst thing you can do. You and your wife will always have problems if you do. I have been with my wife for forty-four years, and believe me, times have been hard for us both. But I made a vow to her and God to forsake all others against her. Your mother is your mother, and will be that for the rest of your life, but your wife is a gift from God. The bible says, 'For this reason a man will leave his father and mother, and be united to his wife, and the two shall become one' (Ephesians 5:31). Darius, there is an alignment that married people must follow. First it's Christ as the head, then husband, wife and children, but to fully understand those principles your household must be in order. You as the husband and provider of the family need to be aligned with God's word. If not, it's not going to work, son. I will be praying for you and your family, but remember what I said. Forsake all others, and pray with and for your wife, as well. If you need someone to talk to, I'm here. But find positive men who will pour into your life and marriage, not those who continue to cause chaos and confusion. Acquaint yourself with Christian couples. It truly makes a difference. You and Symone have had a difficult road. You have both made mistakes, but you chose to forgive each other and work on your marriage. Don't let anyone, family or friends, come between what God had joined together. Do you understand me?"

"Yes, sir, I do. And thank you Mr. Hollins."

"You're more than welcome, son. And let's make plans to go out to dinner with our wives soon. Be blessed, Darius and love your wife the way God wants you to. I'll be praying for you both."

Darius had put the phone on speaker so Symone could hear and speak to Mr. Hollins, as well. She was elated that someone had finally gotten through to Darius about the meddling of Gertrude, and she could only hope and pray that this time he would listen.

After Darius ended the call with Mr. Hollins, Symone proceeded to the kitchen to prepare a large breakfast for her family. She was still so sleepy from the argument with Darius last night, but Jordan had to be at school early for band practice, and she had to get ready to go to work.

Symone looked forward to returning home later that evening, taking a hot shower, and crawling back into her bed. After breakfast, Darius decided to lead his family in prayer as they went their separate ways.

Later that evening, Symone decided to call and invite her husband to lunch. She was so glad that he had spoken to Mr. Hollins, now the ball was in his court to protect his family.

"Hey baby! How's work?"

"Hey honey. I decided not to go to work today. Momma called to see if we could spend some time together before she leaves for tomorrow."

"Oh okay. Well enjoy yourselves, and I'll see you when I get home. Love you, hubby."

"And I love you, too, wifey."

Symone wasn't too pleased to hear this news, but after the conversation that transpired this morning, she felt somewhat optimistic that Darius would start to see things from her point of view. She still couldn't understand this hold or neediness that Darius had when it came to Gertrude. Sometimes Darius would act like a little boy needing his mom's approval and attention. It didn't matter that he was almost fifty years old. It just didn't make any sense to Symone.

Symone's day was long and exhausting. What she yearned for was a hot shower and sound sleep.

After leaving work, Symone got a call from Darius while she was on her way home. "Hey baby. Shoot, I forgot Jordan has swimming lessons."

"I'll take him," he said. "Momma and the kids want to see him swim. After that we will probably go to dinner. Is that okay? And just to keep confusion down I don't think you should come with us."

Symone knew she was tired. Maybe she was hallucinating, but her husband did not just tell her she couldn't go to her own son's swimming lessons. Did he?

"Excuse me?" Symone asked, irritated. "What did you just say?"

"Baby, to keep everything cool, I'll take Jordan to practice."

"Darius, are you crazy? Do you hear yourself right now? I'm going to hang up this phone right now."

All that was left to hear was a dial tone in Darius ear.

"Is he crazy?" she lamented. "This is the type of foolishness I have to deal with when Mommy Dearest comes to town. Did he not remember what we talked about basically all night long? And he thinks it's okay for him to shut me out when his Mommy is here? Oh no! Lord, is this marriage even worth saving? I'm tired of the constant headaches and the never-ending tears. But most important, I'm so tired of bargaining with him to keep peace in my mind and my home."

After that demeaning phone call, Symone decided to pick Jordan up from school and take him to swimming practice herself. She didn't care what Darius, his mom, and his children thought of her. When they arrived at the house, she told Jordan to get ready for swimming lessons. Moments later, she heard Darius pull into the driveway. Symone knew that Gertrude and his children had to be in the car with him. Darius came into the house asking if Jordan was ready yet.

"Darius, I will take Jordan to practice today, don't you worry about it."

"What do you mean? Symone, I told you that Momma wanted to see him swim."

"Look Darius," Symone responded, very irritated. "How dare you tell me that I can't go watch my child swim because your mother does not want me in her presence? Have you lost your ever-loving mind? Like, I said, I will take Jordan to swimming practice and you can go with your mother and children to dinner. I got this."

"So, what am I suppose to tell my mother and kids, Symone?"

"Honestly, Darius, I don't give a flying frog what you tell them. I just don't care."

"Symone, you're being unreasonable."

"Bye, Darius. I'm done with you and this senseless conversation."

"Symone, I am not done talking to you."

"Well dear, I am certainly done talking to you."

Jordan ran into the living room with tears in his eyes. "Mommy! Daddy! Can you please stop arguing?"

"I'm sorry, honey," Symone whispered to Jordan. "Let's go."

And off Symone and Jordan went.

CHAPTER 28
Regrets

Serves me right for falling in love with a married man. I mean, they haven't been together that I know of for over two years, but that could be a lie, too.

After that dreadful phone call, Alani packed her things and ran out of Brexton's apartment in tears. Brexton tried several times to explain that his soon-to-be ex-wife Liza was just being spiteful and trying to get into Alani's head. She didn't care. She just wanted to get far away from Brexton, his wife, and this entire ordeal. He continued to call Alani during the night and all the next day, but she ignored his calls and his presence at work.

Alani knew that she had to get out and clear her head, so she decided to call her friend Cha'relle, who was always ready to have a good time. "Hey girl. What are your plans for tonight?"

"Hey, Alani. A couple of friends and I are rolling out to this new club called the Megadrox. It's the hottest spot now. What's up Alani? Brexton gave you permission to go out?"

"Permission? Girl please! I'm not married to Brexton."

"Shoot, I can't tell," Cha'relle replied jokingly. "Girl, you never hang out with us anymore since Brexton followed you. All you do is stay cuddled up with him. Although we both know he is a married man. But you're still my girl and I love you."

"Char'elle look, I don't want to talk about Brexton tonight, okay? If it's not too much to ask, can you come by and swing me up? I'll be ready in about an hour."

"All right, Alani. Will do. I'll see you soon, girl."

Alani knew the Megadrox was the hottest club in town, and it was a dress-to-impress atmosphere, so she knew she had to step out looking good. She spent several minutes in her closet trying to choose the correct outfit. She decided on a white one-shoulder jumpsuit that had a split on each side. Yep, this will do. She smiled and admired her outfit, and paired it with her new Badgley Mischka strap heels. Alani jump into the shower quickly the hot water drops felt so good hitting her skin, she decided to use one of her favorite peppermint body scrubs by A Nu'u. This product would keep her body tingly and moisturized all night long.

Just then she heard her doorbell. "Oh no! I'm not even ready yet." Alani jumped out of the shower, wrapped herself in one of her plush extra-large towels, and ran to the door.

"Who is it?" she asked.

"It's Brexton, baby. Please open the door."

Alani was not in the mood to deal with Brexton right now. He was the one she wanted to escape from.

"Brexton, now is not a good time. And honestly, I'm not ready to see you just yet," she answered through the door, very irritated.

"Alani look, I'm sorry for what happened at my place. I told you my wife was crazy. She would do anything to jeopardize what we have."

"And that's the problem. You're still married! Look Brexton, I have got to go. We will talk some other time. Good Night!"

"Alani," Brexton shouted through the door. "I'm not playing with you, and I will not be dismissed like a child. Now, I'm telling you to open this damn door!"

Alani had never known Brexton to raise his voice at her like that. Honestly, she didn't know what to expect.

"Alani, I will stay out here all night if I have to, until you decided to open this door."

"Brexton, go home. It sounds like you're drunk anyway. Please leave me alone."

Okay, Alani. Remember I have a key, and no chain nor lock will keep me from breaking this door down. So we can do it one of two ways. I can stay out here all night, or I can break the door down."

Alani began to become fearful, for she knew then that this was the dark side Liza had referred to. Alani continue to plead with Brexton to go home, but he refused.

"Please, don't make me call the police."

Just then, she heard Brexton crying on the other side of the door, pleading with her to forgive him, and confessing his love for her.

Lord, I don't feel like dealing with his crap. What am to do with his man?

CHAPTER 29
Broken Pieces

When Symone and Jordan returned from swimming practice, she found Darius sitting on the sofa with a distinct look on his face talking on the phone. "Okay mom she's here now, I have to go."

Symone instructed Jordan to go shower and get ready for bed. Darius looked at Symone with a look of disgust on his face.

"So, now you refer to me as 'she.' Unbelievable," she muttered.

"Symone I was talking to my mother, and yes I referred to you as 'she' instead of another choice of words that I could use."

Symone felt her temper rising, but she knew she had to remain in control. Darius knew how to use tactics to make her lose her temper, yet she was determined not to give in to his foolishness. "Darius, just leave me alone. As a matter of fact, why are you even here? I thought you were going to eat with Mother Dearest and your children?"

"First, off Symone, this is my house and I don't have to go anywhere."

"Oh! So now it's not ours but yours? The money I have poured into this dark dungeon, the time I've spent remodeling the bathroom, had the house repainted and the fixtures added, that I purchased...not to include the utility bills I help pay for. Now, it's your house? I thought it was ours, Darius?"

"Symone, this is not going to work. We're not going to work. Look how you disrespected me, my mom and my children."

"You! All you freaking think about is you!" Symone screamed at the top of her lungs. "You allow your mom to disrespect me continuously, and you don't say a word. My God, didn't we just go over this last night, Darius? All night we talked about this, and then one day with Gertrude and your mind has flipped again. Seriously, what is it with you and your mom? I feel you are married to your mom, because you sure as hell don't act like your married to me."

"Stop talking about my mom, Symone, I'm warning you!"

"You're warning me? I don't think so. I suggest you watch who you're talking to, Darius Xavier Jackson. I am certainly not your child."

Before Symone knew it, Darius was standing right in her face. She began to feel uneasy, but she would not let him see her sweat. She would most definitely stand her ground. Symone thought to herself, *What has gotten into Darius?* He was acting as though he hated her.

Darius was staring her down with anger in his heart and eyes were red as a flame. Before she knew it, Darius had pushed her pretty hard against the wall.

Symone immediately recovered from the stumble and was back on her feet. She pushed him back down on the sofa. "Darius," she warned him, "don't you ever put your hands on me again, or I'll—"

"You'll do what, Symone? You already cut me, remember? You're just an evil-ass person!"

"Don't worry, I'm getting the hell out of this house. And you're right about one thing, it's not going to work! Jordan let's go," Symone yelled.

"Oh, you can go if you like, but my son is staying here," Darius replied, cold and dry.

"Over my dead body," Symone answered. "If you think I'm leaving my child here with you, your crazier than I thought."

Darius grabbed a vase from the wall unit. "I swear I feel like knocking you across your head.

"And I promise you, my dear husband, if you do I will meet your soul in Hell."

Immediately, Darius started throwing glass figurines all over the floor, breaking the table lamps, and he didn't stop there. He went through the house, dismantling anything that reminded him of their marriage.

Symone stood back in horror, looking at this man she didn't know. He took the oil painting off the fire place that Symone'd had done for them as a wedding anniversary gift. Within a few minutes, he'd destroyed all their wedding pictures and frames. Darius had turned their entire house upside down, leaving broken glass everywhere.

Symone heard Jordan yelling from the hallway, "Daddy stop! Please stop."

Darius ran to his son, telling him that he couldn't be with his mom anymore, and he was leaving.

Symone followed Darius to their bedroom, pleading with him to stop and apologizing for everything, but this only angered him more. Symone looked right in Darius's eyes, but all she saw was coldness and rage. She knew that the man before was not her husband. She looked him directly in the eyes and cried, "Demon Get Out!"

Darius looked at Symone like a mad person, then burst into laughter. "You sound pathetic, girl. Now get the hell out of my way."

Symone refused and continued to block the door so he couldn't get out. Darius pushed her into the wall, but she caught the fall and continued to block the door. He pushed her to the floor, hard, and shook her vigorously, but she knew once he left the house, their marriage was over.

The sound of a beeping car horn came from the front yard.

"Symone, I have had enough. My mother and children are here, and you better move out of my way. If I have to climb out this window, I will. Get the hell out of my way, or you will get hurt."

"Darius, baby, please," Symone cried. "Look at what you've done to us."

"Symone, we were done when I said, "I Do."

"Is that truly how you feel Darius? After all the heartache and pain you have put me through, ex-wives, your cheating, your disrespectful children and a mother in-law from hell? I married you despite the naysayers and your drama! I still chose you!"

"Well now, Symone, you can be free like the wind. I'm not going to tell you again to move."

Just then there was a knock on the front door. She knew there was nothing more she could do, so she moved from the doorway and asked her husband to pray with her, pray that God would intervene now more than ever in their marriage.

As they stared at one another, Symone thought there was a breakthrough, but then came another knock on the door. Symone then ran to the door, and it was his daughter, Damisha.

"Is my daddy ready?" She was looking at all the glass and broken pieces on the floor.

Darius yelled out from the bathroom, "I'll be right out sweetheart," without a care in the world for how he had destroyed the house and their marriage. Darius walked past Symone, but she grabbed his shirt pulling him with all her strength.

"Darius, don't do this please!"

But he managed to open the front door, and there on the front porch was Gertrude and his son Dyon. Symone let go. She knew right then that no matter how much she loved and wanted their marriage, his mother would always be the main woman in his life.

Symone felt overcome by rage at him and the hell he'd put their family through. She began throwing whatever she could find at Darius—his military awards, trophies, and a flower pot that was by the door.

"Get out!" she screamed.

Jordan came up behind her, crying and screaming, "Mommy don't!"

She turned to see Jordan picking up the broken wedding picture frames and glass in his hands, trying to put the torn wedding pictures back together again.

"Look mommy, I can fix it!" he cried, brokenhearted.

Feeling like a fool, Symone grabbed her son and held him as tight as possible in her arms while both began to cry. They stumbled into the house and collapsed, weeping until they cried themselves to sleep. After what seemed like a nightmare, Symone woke up on the sofa with the glass still all over the floor, and she knew it wasn't a nightmare but her life. She knew that something had to be done. This was the first time she was afraid of Darius, and she didn't know what else he was capable of.

But to see her son in so much pain hurt her even more.

Symone picked up the phone and dialed. "Hello, I need to file a report of domestic violence and request a protective order against my husband."

CHAPTER 30

The Promises of God

After the police came and viewed the damage in the house, they also took pictures of Symone's arms and legs which had several bruises due to Darius pushing and shoving her against doors and the floor. When the cops left, Symone went into the bathroom, closed the door, and fell to her knees. The only name she knew to call was Jesus. She knew that this was too much for her to carry. It felt as though she was drowning in this marriage, and the more she cried and yelled, no one heard her. Especially not her husband. Symone had never experienced this type of betrayal and pain. She and Darius had been in bad places with each other before, but never had Darius rejected her and Jordan. She didn't know if this was how he really felt, or if Gertrude was the snake leading him away from his wife and son. She couldn't believe this was her life now. She and Darius had always made it through whatever life had thrown at them...at least, that's what she had always thought. Until now.

Symone felt the man she saw last night was possessed. She had never seen evil up close until she'd looked into Darius's eyes. *What is this spirit Lord that got my entire body and home unsettled?* she pleaded. She began to recite bible verses that brought comfort and strength for her soul, but to also protect her and her son from any evil that might be dwelling amongst them.

"No weapon formed against me shall prosper" (Isaiah 54:17). "The Lord is my Sheppard I shall not want" (Psalms 23). "But the Lord is Faithful he will establish you and guard you against the evil one" (2

Thessalonians 3:3). "God is our refuge and strength in the time of trouble" (Psalms 46:1).

Symone began to let those verses meditate in her spirt, for she knew that the fight was not against flesh and blood, but of evil spirits, and now that spirit had shown its head. Once she got up from the bathroom floor, Symone began to write these verses on Post-Its, and posted them all throughout the house. Then she took her oil, prayed over it, and anointed herself and Jordan in the name of the Father, Son, and Holy Spirit.

"Heavenly Father, please keep me and my son covered by the blood of Jesus, and also Darius. Whatever this demonic spirit is that's attacking this family, we need you to shield us under your wings and build a hedge of protection around us. Amen."

It took Symone four days to clean the entire mess of broken glass and damaged items. Symone and Jordan went to stay in a nearby hotel for a couple of days until she could decide what to do next...or if she even wanted a life with her husband anymore.

CHAPTER 31

Let Him Go!

After pleading with Brexton for approximately forty-five minutes through the door, he finally agreed to go home. But only after Alani agreed to not give up on them just yet. Soon after, Cha'relle called to inform her that she was pulling into her apartment complex. But after dealing with Brexton's nonsense for over an hour, she was in no mood to go clubbing. *Damn him for ruining my night!*

Cha'relle came to the door looking sexy as ever with her short black jumpsuit and thigh high boots. "Girl! What is the holdup? We're ready to go." Cha'relle must have seen the tears in her friend's eyes, but she didn't judge or scold her. "One question, that's all. Is it Brexton?"

"Yes," Alani whispered, feeling broken.

"Alani, I say this because I love you. It's time you let him go. You have made this man practically your whole life. Sweetie, you stopped having fun. We don't go out anymore and you stopped hanging with your girls. Listen, when you're not with him, he makes you feel guilty. I know you love him, but my friend, he belongs to someone else. His wife. Alani, not only are you playing with fire, but also a covenant."

Alani had never thought about it like that.

"Look, the girls are waiting downstairs. You have two choices. Either you can sit here and dwell on Brexton's feelings, or you can get up, finish getting dressed, and go have some fun. Alani?" Cha'relle said boldly with a crazy grin on her face.

"Okay, girl. Give me fifteen minutes."

CHAPTER 32
An Empty Heart

The next couple of days were hard for Symone and Jordan. After contacting her lawyer Cynthia, and informing her of what had transpired, they decided to meet downtown in Cynthia's office. Cynthia took more pictures of Symone's bruises and expedited the family protective order from the court. Both had to appear before a judge the same day, asking him to grant their petition.

The judge ordered that Darius evacuate the premises immediately, and he was to stay at least one thousand yards away from Symone and Jordan. The order also included a non-contact clause, which meant that all communication between them had to cease until they went back to court. Darius would be escorted by law enforcement to pick up any belongings that he needed from the house.

After returning home from downtown, Symone's emotions were all over the place. She hated that their marriage had to come to this, but she knew it was for the best. After all, Darius's behavior was unlike anything she and her son had ever seen before. For two nights straight, Darius rang Symone's phone. Everything in her wanted to pick up, but she knew the order said no contact, and she didn't know if he was remorseful for his actions and wanted to apologize, or just yell and curse her for taking out the restraining order. So she just let it ring.

Symone was the human resource manager at a logistics company, and her work could be quite demanding. Since the ordeal with Darius, her work had gotten behind. Some days she tried to bring work home with her to complete, but she would end up getting emotional all over again. She decided to confide in her boss Tom about the situation when he inquired about the bruises on her arms and the darkness under her eyes. Symone had always come to work professional and in high spirits before this. The company had recognize her talents and she'd begun to climb the corporate latter quickly. Tom proposed that he would bring someone in to assist Symone until everything was back to normal. Symone knew that many people depended on her, but recently she'd felt as though someone had ripped her apart. And honestly, that was exactly where she was in her marriage—broken to pieces.

Slowly, day by day, Symone felt as though she was getting stronger and stronger. It had been over a month since the fiasco at the house, the last time she had seen Darius. Through all the brokenness and betrayal, she continued to pray for their marriage, herself, and Darius. God was the only one that could mend these broken hearts and a broken home.

After getting ready for bed, her friend June called. "Hey girl, how was your day?"

"I'm doing good. Just about to get into bed."

"Oh, I'm sorry. I didn't mean to disturb you."

"Girl please, we disturb each other all the time." They both started to chuckle. "Anyway, what's up June?"

"I think— No, let me change that. I know your husband has lost his ever-loving mind!"

"June, what are you talking about?"

"Symone, when was the last time you logged into ya'll's joint Facebook account?"

"Honestly girl, I forgot all about that page. Why?"

"I need you to login now and call me back when you're done. But before you do that, my friend, go fix yourself a drink. You're going to need it. Call me back, Symone. I mean it."

Symone didn't know what she was going to see, but after that quick conversation with June, she knew that it had to be bad.

Logging onto their social media page, before her very own eyes were Darius and some cheap thrill all hugged up in an intimate setting.

Symone almost dropped her glass of merlot at the sight. Skeptical, she continued to scroll the page, and saw more pictures of these two... along with negative comments from Darius pertaining to his marriage, using all sorts of vulgarity. Each slanderous comment had a follow-up from Gertrude and his new cheap troll, who wore a pound of make-up and a not so fresh weave down her back. This type of female, Darius had never been attracted to before. Then again, nothing was what it once appeared. Symone felt her heart pounding excessively and a migraine coming on fast. Here she was, praying and fasting for their marriage, and there he was, out committing adultery in plain sight for all to see.

Just then the phone began to ring. She knew it had to be June, but Symone sent it to voicemail. She'd begun to feel like a complete fool, embarrassed and ashamed for loving a man and believing in their marriage, only to be ridiculed and slandered all over social media.

Symone soaked her bed with her salty tears once again for the pain and sorrow, and for her marriage which felt like death. At that moment she would welcome death, to erase all the agony within.

Hours later in the middle of the night, Symone awoke with a sudden urge to write. She grabbed a notebook and a pen from her nightstand, and began to write. The words just started to flow onto the sheet of paper...

Time to Move On

Eleven years of laughter, smiles, tears and craziness too.
Eleven years of plans and commitments to always stay true.
Eleven years we've prayed together, stayed together, and yes also laid together,
But the best gift of all was our beautiful son we made together.
We said we could make it through the storms and the rain, but when the storms came, you felt ashamed.
The day we became one was always a dream come true,
Many said we wouldn't make it, but I believed and trusted in you.

But then the gossip, enemies, and harlots came, and you refused to stand on marriage and its sacred name.
For you were taken by the streets, the lust, and blindness of another,
You forgot all about our son and his mother,
You continued to spread your lies, and never admitted to your own faults,
But that's okay, God's got me and our son, and we're never alone.
So, my dear, choose the streets, the games, and the lies they tell, but believe me when I say, "It is well; It is well."
Times are hard, and the struggle is real;
Real for you to know, indeed, Life Lessons are for real!
There was always an alignment for three and alignment from God to you, then me,
But now the alignment has been broken and the vows you promised are gone.
I wish you well, my love, but heaven and I finally know it's time to move on.

CHAPTER 33
Decision Time

Alani stomach felt very uneasy as she sat across from Brexton at the Golden Fish Grill. Brexton had called Alani early Sunday morning inquiring when they could meet. For a moment she'd forgotten she had agreed to meet with him, but after that tantrum last night she would have agreed to anything to get him away from her door. Alani felt trapped and pulling herself into two directions. One part wanted to leave Brexton, but the other part wanted to be totally his—mind, body and soul.

Her thoughts started to drift. *What would happen if I decided to stay with him?* she thought. *Would we truly be together? I know that I love him more than I could have ever imagined. He gives me the world. Anything I need or ask for he provides. Then again, he is married with a family.*

"Alani, are you there, sweetheart? Did you hear what I just said?" Brexton asked, but he knew her mind was somewhere else. "Please Alani, this is very hard for me to say. I need to know if your paying attention to me."

"Brexton, I'm sorry. Please continue what you were saying." But by that point she had no idea what Brexton was saying.

"Look, I know I am married with a family, and sweetheart, when I first met you overseas, honestly, I was just looking for sexual gratification. But the more time we spent with each other, the more I found myself drawn to you. I never meant to fall in love with you. And yes, I admit I have been with other women during my marriage. But you have changed my life. I want to be with you and only you. I can feel you pulling away from me, and it scares me. That's why I freaked out and acted crazy. Alani, I feel that I'm the one who has the most to lose here. This divorce is taking longer than I ever thought, and the hardest part for me is walking out on my children. Liza and I have been over for some time now. There is no love there at all. Please believe me, I'm trying to reassure you. What else do you want me to do? I love you Alani."

"Brexton, I don't know. I'm so confused and torn inside. I never thought of myself as a side chick. I never wanted another woman's husband. I want my very own husband and family someday. Brexton, I too was blindsided by this relationship. I didn't want anything serious. In the beginning, it was a game to see if I could get your attention. But I got more than that...I got your heart. I need some time to sort things out. I need some space for myself. If we decide to move forward, I don't want to have any regrets. But most important, I don't want you to resent me later for your choice regarding your family. Can you accept and respect my wishes, Brexton?"

"Alani, if that is what you desire, I will respect your decision. Just know that I love you more than my very own life."

CHAPTER 34
Who Are You?

After dinner, Alani followed Brexton back to his place to retrieve some of her clothing that was in his closet. She really didn't want to stop by his apartment, but her closet had started to look bare, and she remembered a while ago she had asked Brexton to pick up her clothing from the dry cleaners. That was over two months ago. After retrieving her clothing and some toiletries, Alani softly kissed Brexton good-bye. When she saw tears swelling up in his eyes, her heart began to melt as she stood before the man whom she had grown to love very deeply. As Alani walked pass Brexton, he grabbed her by her arm, tightly squeezing it.

"Brexton, you're hurting my arm. Please let go."

"Alani, I can't allow you to do this," he replied.

"What do you mean, you can't allow me?"

"Baby, please listen. Why can't you see how much you're hurting us, and what you're doing to me? I'm prepared to leave my family for you!"

"First off, I never asked you to leave your family. As I recall, you told me you were separated two years ago. So Brexton, what is the truth? Or have you been lying to me for the last two years?"

"Alani, that's not what I meant."

"Oh no! That's exactly what you meant to say. But please don't worry, Brexton. If I didn't know before, I surely know now. This cannot work," she cried.

Suddenly, Alani felt a powerful blow to the side of her head. Her temple started throbbing and she fell backward and stumbled against the closet door. It took her a moment to realize what had just happened. After regaining her composure, she stared at Brexton who had a look in his eyes that was full of rage. She no longer recognized the man who hovered over her. Without thinking, Alani grabbed a marble candlestick from the coffee table and struck Brexton across the forehead. He fell backward, landing directly on the glass table, shattering it into a thousand pieces. Brexton was out cold.

Alani fell to the floor and huddled in a corner crying uncontrollably. She couldn't believe that he'd hit her, the man she had loved for over two years. He had just broken the love and her heart within a few minutes. Alani knew she had to do something, call someone, but who? She picked up the phone and dialed the only person she could confide in at this time.

"Granny," she cried hysterically through the phone. "He hit me!"

CHAPTER 35
Just Foolishness

The judge ordered that Symone and Jordan could reside in the family residence until the next hearing, which would be within the next hundred and twenty days. Darius was not allowed back into the home. But after seeing Darius's infidelity all over social media, Symone knew that she no longer wanted to live in this house. Even though she loved the tenants in her old house, she had to contact her Realtor to inquire if they were interested in terminating their lease agreement early. It was time for Symone to take her child and move back home.

After conversing with her Realtor Debra, she discovered that her tenants had planned on moving out the following month, so they were not going to renew their lease. This was a sign Symone thought to herself. It was time to go home.

Symone asked some of her co-workers to come and help her move. She didn't have family in Savannah, so she relied on a few of her friends to help. Many questions started to circulate in the office regarding this request, but for her sanity and Jordan's welfare, she had to leave this place they'd once called home. As Symone packed her things in the vehicle, she couldn't help but notice that Darius's neighbor Ricky was outside and on his phone, watching her every move. She automatically knew that Darius was on the other end. As a matter of fact, every move Symone made these days, his nosy neighbor would report back to Darius. Symone discovered this when one of her fellow sisters in Christ had invited her to a Women's Event on a Friday night. Symone left her car in the driveway and they drove Leeasha's car to the event.

Later that night she received a phone call from her friend Tamara, who said Darius had called her stating that he didn't want anyone at his house. Symone and Tamara started to laugh at the foolish and childish antics from Darius.

"Lord God, Tamara. I'm at a church event praising God, and he is worried about another man."

The only man that Symone wanted in her life now was Jesus Christ. If only Darius would get ahold of Christ. Wow, how dynamic it would be! But Symone couldn't focus on that anymore.

Slowly but surely, things started to improve. But just around the corner, more heartaches and tears were to be shed.

CHAPTER 36
Home for The Holidays

The holidays were coming up soon, and Symone missed her family in Miami, Florida. She really couldn't afford to go home because money was so scarce. Darius didn't send anything to support Jordan, so everything was on her. But she needed to be around family and feel love, so they went to visit their family, along with Brownie the family dog.

Thanksgiving was always a large celebration for them. They enjoyed being around family and friends. When Symone arrived home, a few of her family members decided to attend a high school football game at Symone's old alma mater later that night. This is what exactly what Symone and Jordan needed in their lives instead of turmoil and tears.

Before she knew it, the time had come to an end and it was time for her and Jordan to return to Georgia.

Symone had one more week at Darius's house before the lights and water would be turned back on at her home. Symone dreaded going back to Darius's house along with Jordan, because she knew it brought nothing but despair and sadness. But she reassured her son that they would be back in their own home very soon.

Symone pulled up onto the driveway around ten o'clock that night. After unloading the car and getting Jordan settled, she walked through the house to make sure everything was okay. After entering the guest room, she saw that a window was left open. She knew she had checked everything before they left. Symone became uneasy and nervous, and she checked the bedroom. Instantly she saw that her jewelry stand was open and all of her expensive jewelry, over seven thousand dollars worth, was gone. She started to panic. *Oh Lord, we've been robbed.*

She then checked Darius's closet and saw that his safe had been left open. That was where he kept his nine-mil handgun. They weren't robbed, this deranged man had broken into the house while she and Jordan were out of town.

Symone continued to search the house to see if anything else was missing. She couldn't tell because her mind was in a whirlwind. She told Jordan to stay still on the couch while she checked the backyard. She tried to open the back door, but it was stuck. Symone pulled and twisted the knob, but nothing happened. She couldn't get out.

"My God, I'm locked in the house!"

Symone started to panic, then to scream. Jordan ran to the back of the house, crying, "Mommy, Mommy what's wrong?"

"Honey, we are locked inside the house. I can't open the door!"

But then the idea came to Symone to get a knife and take the entire lock off the door. And that was exactly what she did. She was able to remove the lock and the doorknob completely.

After peeking outside, Jordan cried hysterically, "Mommy! Our bikes are gone. I left my bike right next to yours, remember?"

After she thought about it, he was right. Their bikes were missing. Symone told Jordan to stand by the door and don't move while she went out to check the backyard. As she walked through the yard she noticed there were two large rusty chains and a huge lock on the wooden gate.

"Dear God, the fool has locked us in!" Symone ran inside to get her phone and immediately called 911. "Police please Help! My husband has violated his restraining order and has locked me and our son in the house!"

CHAPTER 37
False Imprisonment

After the police came and searched the property, they also saw where the large metal chains were put on the wooden gate, and confirmed that the back door had been tampered with from the outside.

"Ma'am, are you okay?" asked the policeman. "I understand that your husband is the one responsible for this horrendous act. It is called false imprisonment when someone locks you in an area without your permission. If it's okay, I would like to get our forensics team on this case. Ma'am, where is your husband now," he asked.

"Sir, I have no idea. But I know that my son and I can't stay here. Darius has violated his restraining order several times. Is there anything you can do to protect me and my son?"

"Let's get the fingerprints from inside and outside the house first, and then we will move to the next step. Mrs. Jackson, is there another place that you and your son can go until we question your husband?"

"We're moving out next week."

"Just to be safe, ma'am, I think it's best if you take your son and check into a hotel for a few nights."

"I most certainly will, and I thank you, sir, for your help."

"Okay, go get yourselves packed, and we will be outside waiting for forensics to come."

CHAPTER 38
Out Cold

After calming her granddaughter down, Momma Bee told Alani that she had to make sure Brexton was okay. Alani began to check his breathing and she felt for a pulse. On the other end, Momma Bee began to pray for healing and forgiveness in this situation, but also for the salvation of Alani and her male friend. After lifting them up in prayer, Momma Bee told Alani that everything would be okay, but she had to leave that man alone. Momma Bee reassured her that God heard their prayers and he would deliver, but Alani had to repent of her sins and ask for forgiveness.

As she and her grandmother continued to pray together, Alani heard Brexton's voice. He was starting to wake up.

"Grandma," she whispered through the phone. "He is okay and is trying to get up."

"Good child, now you get yourself together and get out of there!"

As Brexton struggled to regain his composure, Alani ran out of there leaving everything behind, never to return.

It had been two weeks since that dreadful day at Brexton's apartment, and Alani's phone had not stopped ringing. Brexton called her morning, noon, and night. He even had the audacity to interrupt her during a training exercise. Brexton's irrational behavior started to frighten Alani. She needed to tell someone, but who? She couldn't tell her supervisor, because technically Brexton was still married and this would certainly jeopardize her career.

It had been over three months, and Brexton still had not given up. When she and her friends would go hang out, he would show up, and on weekends she would see his truck near her complex. He had begun making her life a living hell. Alani would come home to find flowers on her doorstep and a card tucked in. She felt as though the walls were closing in on her. She was trapped, and she knew she had to do something, and fast.

Alani called Brexton later that night and invited him to dinner Friday night, in hopes that he would listen to reason. If not, she would have to inform her chain of command of the situation. If she was to go down, Brexton was coming right along with her.

Brexton was elated to hear from Alani. He felt that she had finally given in and realized how much he loved her. For the last few months he was literally a mess. He couldn't eat or sleep, and was totally off his daily routine as a non-commissioned officer in the US Army. He knew his job performance was suffering, but the one thing he wanted was Alani. He hated that he'd struck her. It was as if the fear of losing her had driven him back to the dark place that he absolutely hated. He wanted so desperately to make her love him again, but how? He had spent a fortune on flowers and gifts only to find out later she threw them all in the dumpster. The sleep deprivation was getting to him, and each night was a little worse. So he started to drink to help him fall asleep. Several nights he would drive by Alani's place hoping she would talk to him, but to no avail. It never happened.

But now things would be different. She'd finally asked him to meet!

CHAPTER 39

You've been Served

Symone and Jordan were able to move back into their home. After receiving several messages from her Realtor that Darius had been calling her inquiring about her tenants, she knew she had to tell Debra what was going on. Symone only moved in with a few items: her sofa, clothing, and an air mattress each for her and Jordan. The heavier items would be moved out at a later time. Symone knew Jordan missed his cozy bed, but she also knew that this move was best for them both.

When Symone returned to work she could not function as she had before. Symone received a phone call informing her she had a visitor up front. She didn't know who it could be. Symone proceeded to the front of the building, and there waiting for her was a deputy sheriff. "Ma'am, are you Symone Jackson?"

"Yes, I am," she uttered cautiously.

"You've been served."

Symone rushed back to her office and closed the door behind her. Once inside, she opened the packet, and there before her were divorce papers. Moments later, there was a knock on her door. It was her friend June, coming to console her. The gossip had already started to circulate throughout the office.

"He filed for divorce!"

"I know sweetie, I know!"

"June, I don't understand. I've been praying and fasting. God spoke to me about this marriage a while back remember?"

"Yes, Symone, I do, but also remember that God never gave you a time restraint regarding Him working on Darius. Always remember it's during His time and not ours. My friend, I'm right here with you to help you through this as you were for me. Now, lets get out of here, it has indeed been a long day."

Symone and June walked outside together with their heads lifted high, but once the fresh air hit her face, Symone broke down in tears right there in the middle of the parking lot. June hugged her friend tightly, whispering that everything would be okay.

After an emotional and exhausting day yesterday, Symone decided to take the next day off. She did not feel like answering questions regarding the deputy sheriff incident, or entertaining gossip regarding her marriage. After making breakfast and getting Jordan ready for school, she called her lawyer Cynthia to set up an appointment. Just her luck, she had an opening at noon. Symone dropped Jordan off to school and decided to go by the home she had once shared with her husband to pick up a few more items. Symone still had her bedroom set there, along with Jordan's. She would have to hire someone to move it all soon. As soon as she pulled in the driveway, she noticed the family's SUV was gone. Darius had been ordered to stay away from the home for a hundred-twenty days and not to removed anything until they went back to court. She knew that somehow he or someone he knew had retrieved the vehicle. At this point she honestly did not care. As Symone entered the house, she couldn't help but feel emotional, and sadness started to overtake her. She quickly went into the kitchen and removed all the pots and pans that she had bought, along with the last of Jordan's clothing. Each passing moment, she hated being in this house. The house represented a place of sadness and brokenness that she no longer wanted to endure. She knew that the hundred-twenty-day mark was fast approaching, and that Darius would be back soon. She wanted every item that belong to her out that house.

Since she and Jordan moved out, she had felt no responsibility to pay the utility bills. That was something he would have to deal with when he returned. After retrieving her belongings, she went to her vehicle to put them in the trunk. As soon as she closed her trunk, there in his driveway was Ricky the nosy neighbor. She was pretty sure he was talking to Darius, so she yelled out in a sarcastic voice, "Make sure you tell him I said Hello."

With anger, hatred, and bitterness burning within, Symone felt the need to do something mischievous or just plain evil. *This man has cause me nothing but heartache and treated me like shit, I've had enough!* Symone walked to the backyard, scooped up some of Brownie's poop, put it in a bag, and proceeded to the kitchen. She emptied the poop into the blender, then went into their bedroom. Symone removed four pair of Darius shoes, took a butter knife, and spread dog poop all inside Darius's shoes, and finished it off with a hint of Febreze.

"You want to treat me like shit, now you can walk in it!"

CHAPTER 40
Too Much to Handle

Money had been very tight for Symone these days. The bills kept adding up, and now she had another expense of paying her lawyer to represent her in the divorce case. Work was finally getting back to normal, but now the assistant they'd brought in to help her was now basically doing Symone's job. Although she was glad she was there to help, Symone always knew she had to keep one eye open regarding her career.

Later that night she was awakened by the ringing of her phone. This time it was her mother telling her that her grandmother had died early that morning. Symone felt so guilty because she had not been able to make the trip when her grandmother called a few days ago to ask her to come home. But before she passed, Symone had called her grandmother and they sang one of their favorite songs together. "I Want to be at the Meeting." That was Grandma Bee and Symone's favorite gospel song. She knew that her grandmother had been tired, and ready to go home to be with her Lord. Although Symone's heart ached for her grandmother, she knew she was in a better place. Her grandmother had been the nucleus of the family and the strongest woman she had ever met.

While the salty tears fell from her eyes, Symone whispered into the phone, "Momma, I'm coming home." She hung up the phone and lamented, "Lord, first my marriage, and now my grandmother. I don't understand this. All I know is, it hurts. It hurts a lot."

Symone informed her boss of her grandmother's passing the following day and he was very understanding, for he knew how close Symone was to her grandmother. "Take as much time as you need Symone," Mr. Miller replied. "Take care of your family first."

That night Symone packed her bags along with Jordan's and Brownie's, and once again they hit 1-95 South to say their final good-byes to the woman she held so dear in her heart—Grandma Bee.

CHAPTER 41
Caught Up

After agreeing to meet Brexton for dinner, nothing went as Alani planned or hoped. He could not get past his own feelings and his personal wants and needs. One thing was for sure, Alani had to inform her chain of command immediately of what was transpiring.

That following Monday morning, she sat waiting for First Sergeant Willington to call her into his office. She was nervous as a wreck. She only hoped that this would not jeopardize her career as a U.S. soldier. First Sergeant Willington called Alani into his office. There standing in the middle of the room were her platoon and section sergeants. This was not going to be good…

Sergeant Lovett, we received a very disturbing call from Master Sergeant Nyles and his wife regarding your relationship. Is there anything that you would like to tell us regarding you and the master sergeant?

Alani told her superiors the entire story, from when they met in Germany to the physical abuse, and now to the stalking. Each sergeant looked bewildered because Brexton and his wife had painted a very different story. Basically, they'd claimed that Alani had been flirting with Brexton and she had become fixated on him since they meet in Germany.

Alani couldn't do anything but laugh at the accusations that Brexton and his wife were claiming. But her sergeants didn't find it a laughing matter.

"Sergeant Lovette, I don't know who to believe. But as I told Mrs. Nyles I have seen you driving her husband's truck around post, and I also reassured her that this would be dealt with accordingly. Now, I can't control what Master Sergeant Nyles does, but as your supervisor and first sergeant of Charlie Company, I am giving you a direct order to cease all involvement with Master Sergeant Nyles. Do I make myself clear, Sergeant? And you will be written up by your section sergeant for inappropriate relationships with a senior ranking non-commissioned officer. Now, if you do not have any further questions, you are dismissed."

Alani left First Sergeant Willington office fuming. *How dare they lie about me like that! He and his wife can go straight to hell.* Later that night, Alani was awakened by the loud ringing of her phone.

"Hello?" she answered dryly.

"This is Mrs. Nyles. So tell me sweet Alani, how was your day?"

Alani jumped out of bed. "Lady, are you crazy? How the hell did you get my number?"

"My husband gave it to me. Look, I don't care about you and Brexton, but I do care about his retirement, and I will not allow you to mess that up for me."

"You are freaking crazy. And don't ever call me again," Alani replied angrily.

Click.

The following morning, the entire brigade was to do a five-mile run, and after receiving that absurd phone call in the wee hours of the night, Alani was not in the mood. After completing four miles, Alani started to slow down. It was a cold morning and the wind was blowing extremely hard. Out of nowhere she heard a familiar voice yelling from behind, "Come on Sergeant. You can't fail your soldiers now, can you?"

And there he was, smiling as ever. Brexton Nyles.

"No, Master Sergeant, I can't, and I won't!"

Just the sight of him made her sick to her stomach, but it did boost her energy and gave her the second wind she needed to catch up to her platoon and leave him behind, as she was determined to do.

The rumors had started circulating regarding Alani and Brexton's relationship. In fact, she came to find out that Brexton had started the rumor that Alani was infatuated with him, and his wife was coming to set things straight. Of course, those who knew of their relationship knew that Brexton was lying. Alani realized she had to retrieve her security system footage from her apartment complex, just in case things started to turn for the worse.

Alani couldn't wait for the day to end. She was going to celebrate her birthday all weekend long, and she was going to start tonight, going out with her girlfriends Cha'relle and Jasmine. After work she rushed home for a quick nap before the evening festivities started later that night. Alani put her phone on vibrate so she would not be disturbed while she slept. Three hours later, her alarm started to go off. It was time to rise for the celebration of her twenty-sixth birthday party. Alani checked the messages on her phone. There were five from Brexton wishing her a happy birthday along with other pathetic apologies, and seven from his crazy wife with more threats and vulgarity.

"Okay, that's it! So, you want to call me out and lie about me? It's about time I show you both how crazy I can be."

She knew that Brexton's apartment was about fifteen minutes away. If she timed it correctly, she would be back in time to get dressed and enjoy her celebration as if nothing had ever happened.

Alani pulled into Brexton's apartment complex twenty minutes later. She knew she could get in trouble for this, but she'd had enough of them both and their vicious attacks. She saw that Brexton's truck was not in his parking spot, but along the fence line. She didn't know what she was going to say to them, but it was high time they all met. Alani knocked on the door, but there was no answer, so she used her spare key that Brexton had given her some time ago. Upon entering the apartment, she saw that there were several pots cooking on the stove and a bowl of potato salad sat on the countertop. Alani knew she had to be quick, so she looked around to see how she could sabotage their dinner. She looked under the cabinet to retrieve a bottle of Jamaican Bacardi Rum, one-hundred proof, then she began to pour the entire bottle of liquor into the collard greens that were cooking on the stove. Next, she got the bag of sugar and poured a heavy amount into the potato salad and began to stir, but she didn't stop there. She took the rice and poured the entire carton of salt into that pot. Then she looked in the refrigerator to get some milk, but what she saw was even better. Alani removed the banana pudding from the refrigerator and emptied an entire box of baking soda over the meringue custard. Finally, she opened the stove and retrieved the barbeque ribs from the oven. Alani looked for something else to mix with the meat, and there it was. Two cans of Purina Alpo wet dog food on the floor. She smirked. After opening the cans of dog food, she mixed the ribs with the Alpo and served it on the silver platter she removed from the top of the refrigerator. After ruining Brexton's home-cooked dinner she wrote a note and left it on the silver platter.

Every Dog Needs To Eat! Woof! Woof!

After leaving Brexton's apartment, Alani stopped by his truck. From her back seat she retrieved the bottle of Dawn liquid dish detergent she had purchased, and a bottle of aspirin. She poured some of the detergent out onto the cement and added a little water to the bottle, followed by six Bayer aspirins—for the headaches he had caused her over the years. She shook all the contents together and emptied the entire bottle into Brexton's gas tank.

While driving back to her apartment, she heard Miles Jaye playing on the radio. "I've been a Fool for You."

Not anymore Brexton. Not anymore.

Twenty minutes later, Alani pulled into her complex. Her phone had not stopped ringing.

"Hello?" she finally answered.

"What the hell did you do to my truck Alani?" Brexton yelled at the other end.

"I suggest you ask Dawn!"

Before he could call back, she blocked his number and any others she did not recognize.

"Now, let's go celebrate!"

After celebrating all weekend with drinking and partying, Monday morning had finally come. She was pretty sure that she would be called back into First Sergeant Willington's office for disobeying a direct order, but this time she didn't care. Alani had brought several video clips of Brexton entering her apartment, and of the two of them together. This time she had proof, and it was her insurance to prove to everyone that Brexton was a liar. After lunch her platoon sergeant called for a meeting, and once again she found herself standing in the presence of her supervisors, but this time, First Sergeant Willington wasn't there.

Sergeant Lovette, weren't you given a direct order from First Sergeant to stay away from Master Sergeant Nyles?"

"Yes, sir."

"So please, tell me why I am receiving numerous phones calls early this morning from Master Sergeant and his wife informing me that you broke into his apartment and ruined their family dinner?"

"With all due respect, Sergeant Johnson, I can't break into a place if I was given a key. And besides, I just added some flavor to their meal," she answered humorously.

"This is not a joking matter, Sergeant Lovette. You can get yourself into a lot of trouble."

"Sergeant Johnson, I am sorry that I disobeyed a direct order, but I'd had enough of them. And since no one would believe me, I obtain my own proof. I have video footage of Master Sergeant Nyles entering my apartment numerous times and of us clearly together."

Sergeant Johnson was stunned by the evidence Alaini presented. "I see. Well, I will inform First Sergeant Willington and the Commander of this information at once. But you, Sergeant Lovette, I won't tell you again. Stay away from Master Sergeant Nyles, or I promise you it will be worse. Do you understand?"

"Yes, Sergeant, I understand," Alani replied as she turned to leave the office.

"Sergeant Lovette, the collard greens, though? Rum?"

"Yes sir, the whole damn bottle."

Sergeant Johnson shook his head in disbelief, and chuckled under his breath. "Get out of my office, soldier!"

CHAPTER 42
Saying Goodbye

Many family members had chosen to wear Momma Bee's favorite color, purple, instead of black for the funeral services. Symone started to feel so empty inside. How would she gather the courage to say goodbye to a woman whom she held in the highest esteem? Symone started to reflect on their many days together during her childhood, when her Grandmother would take her to work to clean houses, the many tent revivals that Momma Bee would drag her to, attending several church services throughout the city of Miami, snapping peas on the back porch, picking greens in the garden, or sometimes just sitting around the house talking and singing the gospel.

Now, don't misunderstand. Momma Bee could be mean, as well, Symone would tease others as an adult that she was child abused while growing up. Whatever Momma Bee had in her hand was what you got hit with. Especially those rubber tree switches in the backyard that would never break. Her Grandmother was the strongest woman she had ever encountered. When her grandfather Edwin got sick, Momma Bee never left his side. The same for her sister Pearl. Momma Bee along with other family members, including Symone, took care of and nursed their elderly and sick family members in Momma Bee's home. Even when she joined up and left for the military, she and Momma Bee continued to talk over the phone. So many private conversations that she would always hold dear to her heart.

Unfortunately, slowly Momma Bee had became ill over the years. The disease of Alzheimer's crept in and slowly diminished Momma Bees memory, but through it all she continued to fight. She fought to her very last breath, but was ready for the Lord to bring her home. Quite often Symone would reflect on the times she and Jordan went back home to visit Momma Bee. During one particular visit, Jordan was crying because Symone wouldn't give him a piece of candy. Momma Bee yelled from her sick bed, "Leave that baby alone!" Jordan and Symone went into Momma Bee's room where she laid sick and quite weak. She told Jordan to come over to her. At first, he was hesitant and scared. You must understand that during this time Momma Bee became very frail, but he went over to his great-grandmother as he was told to. She kissed him on the forehead and told him, "You are a good boy," then she began to sing the song "Yes, Jesus Loves Me," and talk to Jordan ever so sweetly.

Jordan ceased crying and told Momma Bee, "I love you," and then ran outside to play.

Symone sat near her grandmother's bedside, and they begin to talk. She whispered to Symone, "Take care of that baby."

Symone reassured her grandmother she would, and now that Symone's life was a constant uphill battle, she clung to her grandmother's words more than ever.

The day had finally come to say goodbye to Momma Bee. Family members from all over flocked in. Many cousins whom Symone had not seen in years attended, and many she had never met; It was amazing how the love of one woman could bring an entire family together. Symone knew that her Grandmother would be pleased, but she was also saddened because it took the death of Momma Bee for the whole family to come together.

The Going Away Celebration was absolutely beautiful, and the church was crowded from the balcony to the bottom floor, so many wanted to say their goodbyes to this devout Woman of God. As Symone sat there surrounded by her family members, she hoped Darius would at least send his condolences by card or flowers to the family. He had become a part of their family, and he knew how close Symone was to her grandmother. Yet, there was not a single word from him, not even a note. Symone requested that the choir sing the song she and her Grandmother sang numerous times together, "I Want to Be at The Meeting," as they escorted the coffin down the aisle of the church.

At the cemetery, Symone looked on as they lowered Momma Bee's coffin into the ground. The tears seemed like they would never stop flowing. A few of her cousins stood together, holding each other up.

"What are we going to do without her?" Symone asked drenched with tears.

"Keep living," her cousin Lamont whispered. "Keep living."

A few days later, it was time for Symone and Jordan to head back to Georgia with Brownie. Before she departed, her mom along with her aunts gathered together for prayer. After the prayer, she was told that Momma Bee wanted her to have the family's rug, as she'd promised so many years ago. So, she and her family loaded the beautiful sapphire blue oriental rug into the truck, along with Momma Bee's bible and some other mementos, and she said her goodbyes.

While backing out of her grandmother's driveway, the tears started all over again. "She never forgot me," she whispered. "She never forgot me."

As Symone put her vehicle into drive, she was flagged down by one of her grandmother's neighbors, Mrs. Joanne. She shared with Symone that she didn't know what was going on in her life, but Momma Bee wanted her to "Trust God, no matter what."

Symone knew that this was her grandmother's spirit reaching out to her and reminding her that God was still in control. Symone thanked Mrs. Joanne and proceeded on, not knowing the next time she would be back home to Miami. The thought of Momma Bee not being there any longer in person was unbearable to fathom, but her spirit would continue to live on.

Back to Work

Symone returned to work the following week. She felt herself getting a little better and smiling a little more. Prayfully, things would change for the better soon. She continued to attend church services and kept herself engaged in prayer. After meeting with her lawyer Cynthia, she was informed that before the divorce would be granted, she and Darius would have to attend mediation to see if anything could be worked out, and also to sign up for parenting class.

Symone knew that the issue of child support would be the biggest issue for Darius, as it had been for his previous marriages, but she really didn't care anymore. She'd always backed him up when it came to his ex-wives ridiculing him, and had even bought his children Christmas clothes when he couldn't afford to, but here he was, dragging her through the mud and breaking her heart as if she didn't even matter.

Later that afternoon, Symone's boss Mr. Miller asked if they could meet by the end of the business day. Symone was hesitant, because it seemed the temp they'd brought in was completing all Symone's assigned tasks. She had questioned her boss before about her lack of workload, but he always assured her that she had nothing to worry about. While Symone prepared to leave for the day, she dialed Tom's extension to see if he was available to meet.

Symone sat there in disbelief as her boss's words floated above her head. Inside, she felt horrified and disgusted as he explained that her job performance was unsatisfactory, and how sorry he was that she was going through a divorce and her grandmothers' death at the same time. He assured her that she would receive severance pay, but that did not eliminate the sting and betrayal she felt at that moment. Symone continued to smile through the bull that uttered from his mouth and thanked him for his time and opportunity. Immediately, she went to her office, packed her items, and left the job she came to love and enjoy.

"Lord, what am I to do?"

Symone had put in several job applications, but nothing had yet come through, and the money was getting low. She cried daily in the shower to hide her tears from Jordan.

"Lord, this is hard. My husband, my grandmother, and now my job. How am I going to provide for myself and my son? Darius's nonsense has cost me the one thing I depended on to take care of us. The constant breakdowns at work, the back and forth to court, numerous police reports, and now I am literally broke. Jesus, please provide for me and my son, because if you don't, I don't know what I'm going to do. Help me Lord. Please! Help me!"

After her prayer, Symone got up from her knees and glanced at her jewelry box, then at her wedding ring. "Lord God, has it gotten so bad that I need to sell my jewelry to take care of my family?" She contemplated for over a week if she could go through with it. There it sat on top of the jewelry box, the wedding ring that she loved so much and the promise she'd made to her dying day. But what good was it now? The vows had been broken and the trust and love was gone. The more she thought about Darius's indiscretions and humiliations, the angrier she became.

"If I must sell every piece of jewelry I have, to take care of my son and keep a roof over our head, so be it."

Hours later, Symone found herself standing in a pawn shop for the very first time.

"Sir, how much for this wedding set?"

CHAPTER 43
Time to Board

It had been three weeks since the episode at Brexton's home, and after submitting all the documentation to her supervisor, Alania had not heard a peep from Brexton. *Finally, I can put all this nonsense behind me and decide on my next move.* Alani continued working hard and focusing on her career as a soldier. On this particular Friday, all soldiers were summoned to their battalions for formation. This rarely happened, and no one knew what was transpiring. Colonel Meeks stood in front of the entire battalion and informed all soldiers that their brigade had been called to deploy to Iraq. So many emotions and fear ran throughout the platoons, including Alania.

"Lord God." she whispered. "We're going to war."

Panic continued to spread throughout Alania's platoon as the words were spoken from their leader. Suddenly the sounds of ringing phones sprang throughout the entire platoon, which was a violation while in formation. Soldiers rushed to turn their phones off because they did not want to get into trouble, but then they heard the word, "Dismissed." Immediately they retrieved their cellphones to converse with the waiting party on the other end.

Alania wasn't sure what was happening, but she saw she'd missed several phone calls from her mom. She called her mom back, shaking and in tears. "Mom what is going on?"

"Alania!" her mom yelled through the phone. "The United States has been attacked! Two planes just crashed into the World Trade Center. Are you okay sweetheart?"

"I am, Mom, but they just told us were deploying. I'm really scared."

Alania did not know what to expect. All she knew was to pray. She prayed for herself, her comrades, and all the families that were going to be impacted because of this war. Training had become vigorous and the hours ran longer in the day. Many soldiers had requested leave so they could visit their families, but most of the requests were declined. Anticipation and nervousness were at an all-time high, and the days were numbered before the entire brigade would deploy to Iraq. Soldiers were given days off to visit with their families when they came to see them off.

Alania's family had come to see her off, as well, and help her pack up her apartment. When it was time to say their goodbyes, the family gathered for prayer and her aunt gave her a cross to wear around her neck as a reminder that Jesus was with her wherever she went. Alania's dad had come to see her off, too. After the hugging, praying, and shedding tears, it was time for Alania and her fellow soldiers to board the plane that would forever change their lives.

CHAPTER 44

We Meet Again

Symone met with her lawyer Cynthia thirty minutes before mediation was to begin. She had not seen Darius in over nine months. Her stomach began to ache. She didn't know what was to be expected, but believed that child support would be a number one factor. Moments later, Symone sat across from her estranged husband and watched her lawyer negotiate the terms of her divorce. Cynthia was not pulling any punches. The entire ordeal was overwhelming and exhausting, and it was costing Symone a fortune. Thankfully, with the help of her family and some short term loans, she was able to afford it all. She had really hoped they would be able to settle without going to court.

As tempers and emotions started to flair, Symone asked for a break and quickly left the room. Symone stepped into the break room breathing fast. Just then her lawyer Cynthia came around the corner.

"Symone are you okay?" she asked in a concerned tone.

"I'm fine. I just needed a minute to myself."

"Okay Symone, but remember why we're here and what's a stake. You are my client and as I told you before, I will fight for you, but I need you to remain calm and focused okay? If this mediation doesn't work, we go to court. So, what I need you to do is drink this glass of water and come back into the room within the next two minutes. Focus, and please don't let your emotions get the best of you, okay? I'll see you in a few."

Symone knew Cynthia was right, but she knew somewhere deep down she still loved her husband. And from the way he was gazing into her eyes, he felt it too. Symone rechecked her makeup and hair in the bathroom mirror. Satisfied with her appearance, she made her way back down the long hallway. As Symone entered the room, all eyes meet her at the door.

"I'm ready to proceed."

Hours later, nothing had been accomplished. As soon as the issue of child support came up, Darius began to disagree with everything that was being requested. Symone couldn't understand why he was being so vindictive. She'd stood by for over ten years and watched him pay for his other children, and their amounts were a lot more than what she was requesting for Jordan. Cynthia and Symone were both becoming agitated by Darius's antics.

"This meeting is over Mr. Darius. My client and I will see you in court. Have a good evening."

The following Sunday at church, Symone could feel the spirit of the Lord within her. She lifted her head high as she was looking into the heavens, crying and releasing all of the negative energy that she had carried in her heart. She couldn't explain what was happening. She remembered jumping around and shouting at the top of her lungs. It was if it was just her and God, and no one else around. Some of the church ushers ran to surround her, but she couldn't stop the tears and the praise. Suddenly, she heard the softest and sweetest voice ever saying to her, "Let it go."

After that encounter, she felt a sense of peace like she never had before. But most of all she just felt happy.

After service, her friend Leeasha ran over to her. "I tried to get to you, Symone, but I couldn't."

"But I saw you, sis. I saw you. Let it go! I don't know what happened, sis."

"You touched Heaven, Symone. The Father has heard you, and released you from all this pain. But believe me, the enemy will try to intercede and deceive you. Be watchful, Symone, and stay on guard. Remember, "The thief comes to steal, kill and destroy." (John 10:10-12) He tried to destroy you, but God said 'No!' Don't let him or anybody else ever steal your joy and happiness again. You are a child of the Highest God, the daughter of a King, and you are what God says you are, no one else. Walk in his presence every day, Symone, for he loves you, and so do I."

Once they got into the car, Jordan looked at his mom and asked if she was okay. She reassured him that she was better than okay.

"That's good to hear, Mom, because I didn't know what was happening. All I know is that you started jumping around and crying. And you hit me on my head."

"Oh, honey, I'm sorry are you okay?"

"Yes, I am, Mom, but it was scary."

"Baby boy, it's nothing to fear. When the Holy Spirit comes upon you, it's a wonderful thing son, it's a wonderful thing!"

Symone didn't know what tomorrow was going to bring, but she knew the Father had heard her once again, and whatever came her way, she and her son were going to be okay.

After pulling into her driveway, her phone began to ring. She saw that it was Darius and sent it directly to voicemail. Later that night, after getting Jordan settled into bed, her phone rang again. *Lord God what does he want?*

Symone answered the phone reluctantly, feeling extremely annoyed. "Darius, Jordan is in bed."

"No, Symone, I want to talk to you."

"About what?"

"Us, Symone. I miss my wife."

CHAPTER 45
Interruption
"Now What?"

"Okay, Darius I guess you have been drinking, so I'm going to end this conversation by saying good night!"

"No, Symone, I am sober. I know what I want, I want my wife and son back home. I messed up badly and I'm sorry."

"Are you serious, Darius? Marriage is not a revolving door that you can come and go as you please. Please remember, you broke our wedding vows, our home and family. And what exactly are you sorry for, Darius? Is it the cheating, lies, humiliation, the divorce, or breaking your son's heart? Which one is it? By, the way does your girlfriend know you're calling your wife?"

"Symone it's not like that, I don't love her. She was just something to do."

Symone couldn't contain her laughter.

"Baby please, listen to me."

"Oh, I'm baby now? I thought it was bitch!" Symone responded sarcastically.

"Symone, I feel as though I'm surrounded by demons. I don't know what's going on."

"Look, Darius, you made your decision. You wanted the streets and now you have them, and as far as something to do, are you serious? You brought your troll into the house we once shared, the house I tried to make a home. You drove her in our family vehicle that I helped purchase, and humiliated me all over social media with your pictures. So please, don't tell me she was just something to do."

"Symone I was wrong and angry at you. I started to listen to what everybody else had to say about us."

"And that's just it, Darius. You listened to everybody else. You gave everybody a say in our marriage except me. Look, we will be divorced soon, so you can continue to do what makes you happy because clearly its not me. Good night!"

"Symone, please don't hang up. Would you consider meeting me, so we can talk?"

"There is nothing to talk about Darius, so I'm going to end this conversation.

Click.

How dare he call me with this foolishness? I can't believe him! First, he cheats, then he files for divorce, refuses to pay child support, and now he wants to talk? Lord God, fix it!

Symone tossed and turned all night. She could not believe the things Darius was saying to her. Was he truly sorry? Or was it another lie?

It didn't matter anymore, because she was finally over him.

But then again, was she?

CHAPTER 46
Far Away from Home

The flight to Iraq seemed like forever. The plane had a layover in Germany for a few hours, then proceeded to Baghdad International Airport. The soldiers, including Alania, were both excited and scared at the same time. After landing that night, the entire brigade proceeded to a nearby camp to process into the country, and for the next five days, life as a soldier started to take it's toll on the soldiers. The heat was beyond unbearable and the constant dust storms were simply miserable. Alania's skin started to burn. Not only that, but she was stuck in the desert sleeping in a tent with at least thirty other soldiers.

Although the soldier's life now was extremely uncomfortable, she still knew she had made the right decision to join the military.

Each soldier was assigned a battle buddy. That meant where ever Alania went, her battle buddy, Jessie, had to go, and vice versa. If Jessie had to go the bathroom, that meant Alania had to tag along as well, and this was the way it would be until the brigade left Iraq. Everyone was accountable for someone else while they were in Iraq.

After five days, the time finally came for Alania's company to depart for their new home for the next twelve months.

The entire brigade settled into a convoy in tactical vehicles to drive across the large, empty desert plains. The ride was horrific and quite scary. Every other vehicle had a fifty-caliber mounted on top of it, ready to shoot at any given moment. Each soldier was instructed to remain locked and ready during the voyage. Alania rode in a tactical vehicle with one other soldier, armed and ready to protect her life and that of her soldier if needed. Hours later, the convoy was instructed to pull over and rest. While one soldier slept, the other kept watch. Two hours later, the shifts would switch.

Before proceeding to their destination, the commander informed the troops that they would be driving through a town, and the locals were not military friendly. He warned them that they might see dead bodies in the streets, and children wandering the areas trying to approach the vehicles. But under no circumstances were they to stop. About an hour later, Alania and the convoy drove through a deserted town and what she saw made her sick to her stomach. Dead bodies lined the streets. The town looked as though it had been burned, but not only that, children were running alongside the vehicles with their hands out, begging for food. Alania looked on with disbelief as the convoy drove through the town with hungry children lagging behind.

CHAPTER 47

Decisions

"Symone, are you really considering meeting him after all the hell he has put you and Jordan through?"

Symone sat across the table listening to her friend June express her concerns about meeting Darius.

"Symone, I don't trust him, and you shouldn't either. How is it when you're finally starting to get your life back in order, he is feeling remorseful? I know he is technically still your husband, my friend, but remember a snake will always be a snake."

"I know, June, but for some reason I feel connected to Darius. I mean, one minute I'm feeling fine, then the next I'm feeling sick to my stomach, but my mind always drifts back to him."

"That's not love, sis, that's a soul-tie, and a very unhealthy one, at that."

"Maybe it is, but I can finally get some closure on why he behaved the way he did, and to know is he truly sorry, June."

"I understand, but we don't always get the closure we desire. I don't like it, Symone, but you're my friend and I'm going to support you either way. If you meet him, just make sure it's in a public place."

Symone agreed to meet Darius at Panera Bread at noon. She of course did not trust him, so that was why she agreed upon a public place, in case things went south. Symone arrived fifteen minutes early so she could prepare herself mentally and spiritually for the encounter.

She decided to have a cinnamon crunch bagel and a large caramel latte for lunch.

Darius arrived in his work uniform and Symone's emotions started to run wild at the very sight of him. But she knew she had to stay in control. Moments passed and neither one of them said a word, but just looked at each other.

"Thank you for coming Symone."

"You're welcome. Now what is this all about?"

"I want to start off by apologizing for my behavior. I was wrong and I'm sorry.

"This is not what I wanted for us and our family, but it happened Darius."

"Please Symone, let me get this off my chest and then you can speak."

Symone listened as Darius went on and on about him feeling neglected and jealous of her career. He also confessed that he was torn between his mother and his wife, and that he let everyone else tell him what to do.

Of course, Symone was not moved because she had heard all of this before. But she saw the tears and remorse in his eyes, and she actually believed he was sorry this time.

After Darius finished, Symone told him how she was tired of Gertrude meddling and him not standing up to protect their family. Then both agreed to write down questions and exchange them with each other. Symone and Darius had to answer each other's questions honestly.

Two hours had passed, and they were now talking and smiling at each other. Darius asked Symone if she would consider delaying the divorce until they were sure it's what they wanted. Darius agreed to do better and not force Symone into anything yet, but he had to end the extramarital relationship immediately, and he agreed.

Upon leaving, Symone and Darius departed with a kiss, acknowledging they would give their marriage one more try. Symone felt that God had answered her prayers regarding her marriage. God had already spoken to Symone before, and told her she couldn't have the marriage she wanted until he finished working on Darius. Maybe that's what God was doing, working on her husband.

Symone felt happy and optimistic. She knew things were not going to magically improve overnight, but she remained hopeful. For the next couple of weeks Symone and Darius met in public places to try and work on their marriage. The time had come for Symone and Darius to be honest with their family members regarding their marriage, and Jordan was the first person who had to be told. Symone wasn't sure how Jordan would respond to the news, if he would be happy or sad about it, so she decided to take him out for ice cream to share the news of his parents rectifying their marriage.

After talking about his day at school, Symone asked Jordan how would he feel if his parents got back together.

Jordan looked at his mom with a confused look on his face. "Mom why would you ask me that? Daddy hurt us, and I don't trust him anymore and you shouldn't either."

"Honey, I know. I've spoken to your dad and he is sorry for what he did. I need you to try and give him another chance. He wants to visit with you tomorrow."

"I don't understand why you're asking me how I feel if your going to do what you want to do anyway. Mommy, I know you're a grown-up, but I'm telling you its not going to work. God already told you to let go. You always tell me to listen to God, and you're not."

"It's not like that, son. I believe your dad is sorry and he wants to make our family work."

"I'll try because you asked me Mommy, but I don't like it. What happens when he makes you angry again?"

"I tell you what. If I feel your dad is going to start an argument with me or get me angry, I will walk away."

"Remember, you did that already and it didn't work."

"I know son. So I'll need your help. If you see me getting angry with your dad, just say 'Mommy let's go,' and we will leave, okay?"

"Okay, but don't let him get you angry again."

"I will do my best. I promise."

"Momma, I don't want anymore ice cream. Can we leave?"
"Are you sure, Jordan?"
"Yes, ma'am, I'm sure."
"I love you son."
"And I love you too, Momma."

Friday, after Jordan got out of school, Symone and Darius had decided to meet at the park. Jordan went off to play basketball with some kids on the court. He didn't know his dad was supposed to meet them there. Darius arrived, and Symone called Jordan over to see his father. Symone could tell Jordan was not thrilled or excited to see him.

"Hey son, how are you?" Darius asked, rubbing Jordan's head and giving him a hug.
"I'm fine Dad. How are you?"
"Good son, now that I see you."
"Okay, can I go back and play, Mom?"
"Sure, Jordan, enjoy your game baby."
"Wow! That did not go as I expected, Symone."
"No, Darius. He is still hurt, and he doesn't trust you."
"I have a lot of making up to do with you both, I know, but please let me try. I love my son and I don't want him growing up resenting me."
"It's up to you Darius, how ya'll's relationship ends. It's just been Jordan and me for some time, and he has seen far too much negativity from us both. This is going to take time, you cannot rush him."
"I understand. What about us, Symone? Have you changed your mind?"
"No, I haven't. This is going to take some time, and honestly, I don't know how long."
"I'm not going anywhere. As I told you. I miss my wife and I want us all back under the same roof."
"Well, time will tell Darius."
"I love you Symone."
"And I love you too Darius."

He embraced her with a soft, gentle kiss right there in the middle of the park, and at that point, nothing else mattered. She and her husband would finally get things right in their marriage.

Three weeks passed, and the time had come for Symone to contact her lawyer Cynthia about delaying the divorce. She knew that it would be a difficult phone call to make, but this was something she wanted to do. Cynthia was not thrilled or overjoyed about Symone's decision. She asked several times if she was sure. Symone reassured her lawyer that she was, and thanked her for her services. After hanging up, Symone started to question herself about her decision. "Five thousand dollars down the drain, just like that. Lord, I hope I'm making the right choice."

Soon afterward, Symone called her mom and sisters to inform them of her decision. No one was pleased, especially her sister. She could sense it in the tone of her voice. After each one expresses their concerns, they all told Symone that they loved her before disconnecting the phone call.

"I honestly feel that no one wants me back with my husband," Symone uttered sheepishly. Symone called Darius, hoping that he would make her feel better.

Darius picked up on the second ring. "Hi beautiful."

"Hello Darius, how are you?"

"I'm okay. Busy as usual with ordering and rearranging stock. How was your day Symone?"

"Not so good. Do you have a few minutes to talk?"

"For you, of course. What's wrong honey?"

"Darius, no one wants us back together, especially not our families, and not even our own son. Is this even worth it? Maybe there is just too much damaged between us and weare just holding onto memories. I honestly don't know what to do. How do we know this time will be different? How do I know you won't step out again?"

"Symone, we both know this is not going to be easy. As I told you before, I will spend the rest of my life trying to make it up to you and our son."

"I love you, but we both know people are going to talk. It's up to us to ignore them and get our family back on track. I let so many people influence my decisions about our marriage, and I don't want to do that anymore. I love you and only you Symone. But the decision is yours. Do you want to try and make this marriage work or not?"

"I do Darius."

"Okay then, that's all I needed to hear, sweetheart."

"But there are some ground rules we need to set."

CHAPTER 48
Mount Up

The battalion and the brigade had finally made it to Baghdad International Airport. The scenery was troublesome and emotional at the same time. Several planes had been blown to pieces and all that was left were shells of what were once airplanes. Upon waiting for word, the battalion was told to dismount their vehicles and meet up front for a quick formation. They were told that the airport had been cleared, and now was a green zone, but they were always to stay at arms and ready.

Alani and some other soldiers decided to explore the unknown territory together. As they walked in and out of condemn buildings, they noticed that the areas had once been the offices of high-ranking nationals. They stumbled upon papers, journals, books and other small artifacts. As Alani continued to walk with the other troops, her mind began to drift to how this area might have looked before the war, and to the people who had worked in these buildings. Four hours later, the brigade mounted back up, heading to an unknown area where they would live for the next twelve months—Camp York.

CHAPTER 49
Bad Intentions

After months spent praying, fasting, and asking God to send Darius home, something still didn't sit well deep in Symone's spirit. She was determined to make her marriage work this time, but for some reason she wasn't sure if Darius was as committed to the marriage as he claimed. Darius was adamant about Symone and Jordan moving back into his house, but she advised him that was not going to happen. She asked Darius if he would consider renting his house out if they agreed to consider starting over in a new home.

This idea did not sit well with Darius. "Symone, how is it going to look? Were married and living in two different houses. This is getting to be too much"

During their talk before deciding to give it another try, both Darius and Symone agreed to not disrespect each other again, either with hurting words or physically. In addition, Darius agreed to start attending church services again with Symone and Jordan, and she agreed that she would apologize to his family. Honestly, she felt that it was straight bull, but to satisfy her husband's request, she agreed to do it. As time went on, Symone and Darius started to drift back into their old patterns. She could tell that Jordan wasn't happy at all, and honestly, she wasn't either. But as a wife and a Christian, she knew she couldn't walk out on her marriage. The only way she would leave was if God released her from it. Only then would she not feel guilty. Darius would spend some nights at her house and she at Darius's. Both had a key to the other's residence and could come and go as they pleased. Symone knew if this was going to work, their marriage had to be rebuilt from the ground up, but Darius never saw it this way.

Symone's birthday and Mother's Day was just around the corner, and she knew that Darius had planned something special, just as he always did around this time. That Sunday morning Symone woke up feeling good, knowing her husband was going to accompany her and her son to church as he had promise. But when it was time to leave, Darius backed out. While at church, once again she went before the altar to ask God to give her a sign regarding this marriage. She wondered if she had disobeyed God by going back to Darius. Honestly, Symone was confused. But little did she know that God heard her prayers yet again, and was going to answer her prayer once and for all. But at what cost?

After leaving service, Jordan and Symone went back to Darius's to invite him to go to dinner with them for Mother's Day. Once again Darius refused, and Symone found herself in tears and torn by his actions.

Darius informed Symone that Gertrude was coming to town and it was up to her to apologize to his mom. Symone reminded Darius that he did not uphold his promise about attending church with her and Jordan, and all bets were off. That Friday evening, Symone found herself back in a place she never wanted to experience again with Darius.

Suddenly, in the mist of havoc and chaos, she remembered her prayer request on Sunday morning. She'd asked God to reveal to her Darius's heart and intentions, and he had done just that. In that instant, Symone knew that her marriage was dead, and that God had exposed Darius's heart so that she could never go back.

She was finally released. Release from pain, negativity, torment, guilt, shame, and fear, yet not by man, but by God himself, and she knew she was going to be okay without Darius and this marriage.

CHAPTER 50

Save My Life Lord

Months had passed and Alani had finally started to settle into her new home in the middle of the desert. For the first couple of months, the soldiers had to conduct personal hygiene by utilizing five-gallon cans, and since there were no easy access bathrooms, portable burn pits had to be built. A burn pit was a wooden porta-john that was used as a restroom, and at the end of the day soldiers were assigned to burn all feces and urine in a black metal can. Not only did they have to actually burn it, but also stir the waste with a long wooden stick. That was one duty all soldiers hated. Since there were no washing machines, each soldier had to wash their uniform by hand. Alani was so happy to receive the washboard her mom purchased for her just before deploying. Although it was rough and tiresome, she was happy she had something to scrub her clothes on to remove all the dirt. Life in the middle of the dessert was extremely hard, but the soldiers continued to build their bonds and each one supported the other. Approximately six months later, they got word that they would be moving inside a building. Everyone was ecstatic because that meant having lights and running water. Little did everyone know it was just an abandoned building.

All platoons were basically kept together, female soldiers on one end and male soldiers on the other. By this time, everyone was getting on each other nerves, Alani found it comforting to keep a journal. It was basically her way to escape the current situation. Occasionally, soldiers were selected to go to another area in the country, "Camp Doha," for shopping and relaxation. This time, Alani and her close friends Cha'relle, Zoya, and three other soldiers were selected to go. Alani couldn't wait to relax at the beach and enjoy a shopping spree, When soldiers departed the theater, they had to leave in civilian attire and Alani knew that it was hot enough to pack two summer dresses and a short blue jean set. Wearing regular clothes was a privilege. It reminded you of who you were when not in uniform. Alani missed showing her beautiful femininity.

Once at Camp Doha, Alani and her friends decided to go shopping at the mall. It was the largest mall in the area, and it reminded them of back home. Jewelry stores, video game arcades, and of course fast food restaurants. Alani burst with a gleam of excitement when she saw Burger King and Baskin Robbins. After ordering their food, Alani and her friends sat down and enjoyed the taste of a hot juicy cheese Whopper, fries, and of course a fresh cold soda. For that moment they felt as though they were back home in the States. After enjoying lunch, the girls decided to go shopping. As Alani passed by the jeweler, she couldn't help but to imagine that beautiful gold herringbone necklace around her neck. It was costly, though she could afford it. But she was determined to watch her spending and concentrate on purchasing a home once she returned Stateside. As they continued to walk the mall, Alani suddenly heard a familiar voice calling out to her. She knew instantly who it was, but she continued to walk even faster, hoping he would give up. Cha'relle knew who it was, but Zoya had no idea why Alani's entire mood had changed. Alani went into a store, speeding through the aisles. The voice continued to follow her. After several evasive maneuvers, she finally hoped he had gotten the message to leave her alone. She exited the store, and around the corner she found herself face-to-face with Master Sergeant Brexton Nyles.

"Brexton, I hoped I would never have to see you again."

"Well, that's funny, because I hoped and prayed that I would see you again."

Cha'relle shook her head in disbelief. "Are you serious Brexton?" she asked sarcastically. "Alani, are you okay?"

"I'm find girl, thanks. Can you give me a minute?

"Sure, take your time, but not too long."

"What do you want Brexton?"

"Alani, please, can you at least give me five minutes?"

"No that's not possible, but I will give you two minutes. That's all. So if I were you, I would start talking."

"First, Alani let me apologize for all the wrong I've caused you. I am so sorry that I hurt you the way I did, it was never my intention. No, matter how you feel about me, Alani, or what I've done to you, please know that I loved you and always will. Now, that I've seen you and I've said my piece, I can only hope that one day that you will forgive me. You've always been a strong person. That's what attracted me to you, amongst a few other things. But you're also a good soldier and I remember how hard you had to fight to prove yourself in Germany to the chain of command. I was so proud of you. So I promise you, my love, that I will never jeopardize your career again."

Alani stood there in shock at the words coming out of his mouth. She knew deep down that he was truly sorry for the pain he had caused her. She hated to admit it, but after all the hell, she still loved him. But it didn't matter anymore.

"Thank you, Brexton, for your apology. I know you're sorry. I truly wish you well in your career and your life, but I must go."

"I understand. Take care of yourself Alani, and if you ever need anything, know that I'm always here."

"About time," Cha'relle said with a smirk. "What did he want Alani?"

"To apologize and wish me well."

"And how do you feel about that?"

"Actually, I feel pretty good. Now let's go get some ice cream."

The day was coming to an end and it was time for Alani and the troops to get ready to go back to Camp New York. Oh, how she'd enjoyed the day out with her friends. And who would have imagined she and Brexton would finally make peace with one another? As the soldiers climbed into the van to depart, Alania was stopped by a soldier she never met.

"Excuse me, Sergeant, I believe you left your bag on the chair."

Oh thank you. I hadn't noticed." She looked in the bag and saw an envelope with her name written on it. She slowly removed the card from the envelope and read it.

Alani, I love you now and I always will. Please accept this as a parting gift from a forever friend. It looks better on you!
Love Always,
Brexton

Alania, removed a gift box of her favorite lotion, spray, and body wash, Cucumber Melon by Bath and Body Works. Brexton had always loved that scent on her. Next, she opened a gold box, and there it was, the beautiful gold herringbone necklace she'd seen at the jewelers less than two hours ago. *How did he know?* she wondered, but couldn't help but smile.

While in flight returning to their camp, the pilot informed them that Camp New York was at Threatcon Delta. That meant there were terrorists attacks in the area, or intelligence indicated immediate danger from terrorist actions. The helicopter had to land in another secure location, and all soldiers were instructed to enter MOPP 4 (Mission Oriented Protective, Posture) which meant that everyone was required to suit up and wear their gas mask, gloves, boot covers, and hoods. All soldiers were always required to carry these items, in case a gas attack occurred. Immediately, Alani and the troops entered MOPP 4. No one was permitted to undress until the signal of all clear was given, which happened much later that night. Alani was informed that their platoon was sending someone to pick them up first thing in the morning, and they should rest until the vehicle arrived.

The following morning Alani and the troops were escorted back to Camp York. As everyone started to settle into their daily routines, the sirens and alarms started to go off once more. Alani happened to be by the vehicles. Once again, all soldiers entered MOPP 4 and jumped in the closet vehicle. Everyone was nervous, but believed in time they would hear the signal for all clear.

Four hours later, everyone was still in MOPP 4. Alani sat next to Staff Sergeant Washington in his assigned tactical vehicle. Specialist Jones and Private Wright were in the rear. To ease everyone's mind, Specialist Jones started singing. He had one of the best voices in the entire brigade. Afterward he asked if he could say a prayer. No one objected to his request. As a matter of fact, they all held hands and asked God to protect them and their fellow soldiers. You could see the fear on everyone's faces and heard it over the radio. The commander reassured the troops that they would be okay, this was what they'd all trained for.

Slowly, Alania noticed that the sky was changing colors. It appeared that they had been gassed. The yellow turned to orange, then blue. This was not normal. Panic started to set in. The Chaplin got on the radio and said a prayer, and all the soldiers started to pray that God would protect them and their fellow soldiers, and save them from what looked to be a gas attack. Another Battalion stood guard around the perimeter, locked and loaded, ready to defend the area at all costs. Alania didn't know if this would be the end for them all, but she knew she had to trust God, and have faith he would not bring her this far to die in the dessert. Alani and the other soldiers in the vehicle shut their eyes, but no one could completely rest with the masks over their faces. But everyone knew they had to stay on. It was hard to stay awake, so they took turns. While two slept, two would remain alert. Slowly but surely, the early morning sun shone through the vehicle, waking everyone up. There was not a hint of color in the sky, just the shining of the sun. The soldiers were given the all clear sign, Some were smiling, some were praying, and others were crying, but no matter what their religion or belief, all knew to give God the praise for sparing their lives.

Alani, smiled with tears in her eyes, thanking the Father yet again for keeping her safe in his arms.

CHAPTER 51
Full Circle

Seven months later, Symone found herself back in court for the final divorce proceedings. This time she was at peace, without a sense of regret, nor was there malice in her heart. She knew she had done all she could to save this marriage, and that was truly enough. As Symone and Lynn waited for the judge to arrive, Symone looked over to her friend and whispered, "I've been here before." Lynn gave her friend a confuse look. "Lynn, I remember sitting in the same exact courtroom on this very bench with Jordan in my arms about ten years ago. I can't believe this, girl. I was here when his ex-wife brought him to court regarding child support. To think I stood right alongside him, defending him. Oh my God! This is crazy, I have gone in a complete circle with Darius."

Lynn's mouth dropped open as she heard her friend's words. "No, Symone, this is not crazy. This is God. Don't you get it? He had to bring you full circle in order that you might see. Think about all the foolishness and pain you've dealt with—foreclosure, repossession, unemployment, arrest, depression, electricity and water cut off, and the list goes on."

Symone thought about all that she had endured while being with Darius. God had not left her, but was leading her out of the wilderness into her destiny. All the hell she had experienced had only made her stronger, wiser, and better.

Lynne continued to chuckle under her breath. "Symone, God had to use this hardship to build you for his Kingdom and his purpose. That's

Grace my friend, Amazing Grace." Lynn started to shake her head. "Now that the blinders are off, Symone, can you see?"

"Huh," Symone replied dubiously. "You know the song, I once was lost, but now I'm found, I was blind but now I see."

"You know I do."

"Girl, things have never looked more clear."

www.ingramcontent.com/pod-product-compliance
Lightning Source LLC
LaVergne TN
LVHW041638060526
838200LV00040B/1622